Books by

CW01650849

Southwestern Shifters

Rescued
Relentless
Reckless
Rendered
Resilience
Reverence
Revolution
Revenge
Reluctance
Renounced
Retrograde

Southern Spirits

A Subtle Breeze
When the Dead Speak
All of the Voices
Wait Until Dawn
Aftermath
What Remains
Ascension
Whirlwind

Love in Xxchange

Rory's Last Chance
Miles to Go
Bend
What Matters Most
Ex's and O's

A Bit of Me
A Bit of You
In My Arms Tonight
Where There's A Will
My Heart to Keep

Leopard's Spots

Levi
Oscar
Timothy
Isaiah
Gilbert
Esau
Sullivan
Wesley
Nischal
Justice
Sabin
Cliff

Mossy Glenn Ranch

Chaps and Hope
Ropes and Dreams
Saddles and Memories
Fences and Freedom
Riding and Regrets
Broncs and Bullies
Hay and Heartbreak
Vaqueros and Vigilance

Spotless

Hide
Hunt
Home
Heart

Coyote's Call

Off Course
In from the Cold
Blue Moon Rising

Valen's Pack

Run with the Moon
Exodus

The Vamp for Me

My Life Without Garlic
Don't Stake My Life on It
Sunshine is Overrated
Don't Drink the Holy Water
The Trouble with Mirrors
That's One Cross Vamp

City Shifters

Bearly There

Yes, Forever

Yes, Forever: Part One
Yes, Forever: Part Two
Yes, Forever: Part Three
Yes, Forever: Part Four
Yes, Forever: Part Five

What's His Passion?

Unexpected Places
Unexpected Moments

Anthologies

Racing Hearts

Single Titles

Breaking the Devil
Lassoes and Lust
Dark Nights and Headlights
Texas and Tarantulas
Belt Buckles and Cowboy Boots
Something Shattered

Chaps and Hope

ISBN # 978-1-78651-894-1

©Copyright Bailey Bradford 2016

Cover Art by Posh Gosh ©Copyright 2016

Interior text design by Claire Siemaszkiewicz

Pride Publishing

This is a work of fiction. All characters, places and events are from the author's imagination and should not be confused with fact. Any resemblance to persons, living or dead, events or places is purely coincidental.

All rights reserved. No part of this publication may be reproduced in any material form, whether by printing, photocopying, scanning or otherwise without the written permission of the publisher, Pride Publishing.

Applications should be addressed in the first instance, in writing, to Pride Publishing. Unauthorised or restricted acts in relation to this publication may result in civil proceedings and/or criminal prosecution.

The author and illustrator have asserted their respective rights under the Copyright Designs and Patents Acts 1988 (as amended) to be identified as the author of this book and illustrator of the artwork.

Published in 2016 by Pride Publishing, Newland House, The Point, Weaver Road, Lincoln, LN6 3QN, United Kingdom.

No part of this book may be reproduced, scanned, or distributed in any printed or electronic form without permission. Please do not participate in or encourage piracy of copyrighted materials in violation of the authors' rights. Purchase only authorised copies.

Pride Publishing is a subsidiary of Totally Entwined Group Limited.

If you purchased this book without a cover you should be aware that this book is stolen property. It was reported as "unsold and destroyed" to the publisher and neither the author nor the publisher has received any payment for this "stripped book".

Printed in Great Britain by Clays Ltd, St Ives plc
1

[illegible]

ISBN 978-1-78651-894-1

Copyright © Bailey Bradford, 2016

Cover Art by Posh Gosh ©Copyright 2016

Interior text design by Claire Siemaszkiewicz

Pride Publishing

This is a work of fiction. Names, characters, places and events are from the author's imagination and should not be confused with fact. Any resemblance to persons, living or dead, events or places is purely coincidental.

All rights reserved. No part of this publication may be reproduced in any material form, whether by printing, photocopying, scanning or otherwise without the written permission of the publisher, Pride Publishing.

Applications should be addressed in the first instance, in writing, to Pride Publishing. Unauthorised or restricted acts in relation to this publication may result in civil proceedings and/or criminal prosecution.

The author and illustrator have asserted their respective rights under the Copyright Designs and Patents Acts 1988 (as amended) to be identified as the author of this book and illustrator of the artwork.

Published in 2016 by Pride Publishing, Newland House, The Point, Weaver Road, Lincoln, LN6 3QN, United Kingdom

No part of this book may be reproduced, scanned or distributed in any printed or electronic form without permission. Please do not participate in or encourage piracy of copyrighted materials in violation of the authors' rights. Purchase only authorized editions.

Pride Publishing is an imprint of Totally Entwined Group Limited

If you purchased this book without a cover you should be aware that this book is stolen property. It was reported as 'unsold and destroyed' to the publisher and neither the author nor the publisher has received any payment for this 'stripped book'.

Printed and bound in Great Britain by Clays Ltd, St Ives plc

Mossy Glenn Ranch

CHAPS AND HOPE

BAILEY BRADFORD

Dedication

To new beginnings and second chances, and those not afraid to grab onto both.

Chapter One

"Wow, I don't know about this," Troy muttered, looking out of the passenger side window. There were freakin' mountains. They made Troy feel small and he didn't like that at all.

"I think it's beautiful," Will said, leaning against Troy. Will, lithe guy that he was, always sat in the middle of the truck's bench seat. Will loved being in the middle, whereas Troy only loved it in certain situations—like when he, Will, and Carlos were all naked and fucking like bunnies. Troy pulled his gaze away from the intimidating ginormous mounds and cast it towards the stoic, chiselled cowboy driving so competently.

Carlos could be a mountain, Troy decided. Their mountain, his and Will's. It had taken Troy a while but he'd come to believe he could depend on Carlos—and Will. Sometimes he thought he was the weak link in their relationship, but he tried not to let his insecurities get the best of him.

"I missed this when we were in Texas," Will continued, and he began to stroke Troy's thigh, just teasing at the inside seam of his jeans. "South Texas is so damn flat, and dry, God, it's awful. Nice people though." Will shifted and nipped Troy's jaw, drawing every bit of Troy's attention then. Will's eyes gleamed with the knowledge that he'd just made Troy's dick so hard he was surprised it didn't drill right through his jeans. Troy knew Will's expressions better than he knew his own.

"Sexy men," Will added, dragging fingers across Troy's rigid length.

"You two gonna put on a show, I might just have to pull

over," Carlos rumbled, and Troy's dick got just *that* much harder. Carlos was still looking straight ahead, watching the road, as far as Troy could tell. He either had awesome peripheral vision, or he knew his men quite well. Probably the latter, Troy thought as he sucked in a sharp breath. Will rubbing his balls was guaranteed to make Troy whimper unless he bit the crap out of his lips.

"We could put on a show for you, Cowboy," Will purred, using his pet name for Carlos. "Or you could pull over and join in, 'cuz I'm gonna be all over Troy and his big dick in just a few seconds."

The whimper Troy had been trying to hold in burst free in a gush of warm air, blood surging through his veins at the promise in Will's voice. Dimly, he was aware of Carlos cursing in that low, rough way he did when he got horny as hell. The truck swerved, bumped along for a few seconds as Will bent and blew on Troy's denim-covered dick.

Troy grabbed a handful of Will's sweet, round ass with one hand and the Oh Shit bar with the other. He closed his eyes and leaned his head back, sliding down as much as he could. Someone—Will, most likely—unbuckled his seat belt, and Troy made another one of those embarrassing sounds as Will unfastened his jeans.

The fact that it was day—a bright, sunny one—rather than night, and that they were out in the open didn't faze Troy at all. After you'd inadvertently made a porn tape, like he and his lovers had back in the bar Troy used to work in, you tended not to be so shy. Troy had never been much on the shy side to begin with, but he really had forgotten about the security cameras in the storage room.

Hell, no one in their right mind would have been thinking about anything other than the two sexy men he'd been with, was still with. A little sunlight and possible exposure wasn't going to stop any of them. Besides, Troy trusted Carlos to take care of them.

There was a subtle scent on the wind, an almost sweet odour that somehow added to Troy's stimulation. Eyes closed, Troy moaned softly at the first flick of Will's tongue over his slit. Everything else ceased to register when Will sucked his crown into the tight, wet confines of his mouth.

Troy's worries along with his doubts and insecurities melted away under the skilled tongue and hard suction. He heard the metallic sound of Carlos' seatbelt being unfastened then the grunts and murmurs as Carlos moved to lean over Will. His mouth was taken and ravished by the expert kiss Carlos laid on him. Troy quivered and keened as his balls drew tight.

"Not so quick," Carlos growled against his lips, following the command with a bite on Troy's lower one. "Got us pulled over in a nice, private spot. No reason to rush this."

Troy would have begged to differ. He was desperate to come. Even so, even lost as he was in his own needs, he knew Carlos would have his way. Mainly because Troy and Will wanted him to.

"Mmm," Will hummed as he sucked Troy's cock in deeper.

Troy gasped and Carlos was on him again, plundering his mouth in a kiss that was every bit as good as being fucked. Troy managed to get a handful of Carlos' shirt, scraping his blunt nails over Carlos' chest as he did so. His other hand he kept on Will's tempting ass.

Will's mouth was divine, but Troy wanted more. He needed to thrust and fuck and be taken—he needed to be in the middle now. None of his fears could slip into his head then, when he was being loved on like that.

Will bobbed down and took Troy in to his throat. Troy jerked his head aside and yelped, struggling not to squirt like a virgin getting his first blowjob. He let go of Will's ass to try to grab the base of his own shaft. Will swallowed and Troy kicked his feet, forcing his climax back through sheer determination.

"Want in," he panted, and hoped to God his partners understood. "Fuck me," was the best he could get out to possibly clarify his needs.

Carlos got it, though, and Will must have too, because Troy, big, muscle-bound guy that he was, found himself pulled out of the truck shortly after hearing the door open. He prised his eyelids apart as soon as his feet hit the ground. Carlos burned him with a hot look then cupped his jaw firmly, almost painfully. He slanted his mouth to Troy's again and kissed him with a savage intensity that made Troy quake from somewhere deep inside all the way out to his toes.

Meanwhile, Will pulled on his jeans, shoving them down. "Lift your foot." Will tugged, and Troy did so. He was melting under Carlos' onslaught, unable to truly focus on anything else.

Until a slippery hand stroked his cock, smearing it with lube. Troy jolted, eyes flying open as Carlos spun him around. His own hole was rubbed, slicked up while at the same time Carlos nudged him towards Will's sweet bottom. Will was bent over the seat, propped up on his elbows and peering eagerly over his shoulder. His pucker glistened and gaped just enough that Troy knew he'd stretched himself, and Troy could just shove in and fuck until he shattered.

Troy took Will's ass cheeks in hand and spread them apart. He noted the way Will's nuts were already pulled up right before Carlos growled at him to get on it.

"Yeah, what he said," Will panted, reaching beneath himself to palm his cock.

Troy didn't need to be told twice, although thinking was becoming difficult what with Carlos pushing a thick finger into his ass. Carlos' hands always looked long, lean, his fingers almost delicate despite the scars on them—and yet, when Carlos slipped a finger into Troy's ass, it felt like he was being opened up with something a helluva lot bigger. Troy moaned, his pucker burning around the intrusion.

Carlos muttered something unintelligible and pushed another digit in. "Come on, honey. Can't fuck you until you get on in Will, and look at Will. He wants you to fuck him so bad, so hard and long. Gonna have to slap that ass a few times while you're riding him."

"Ungh, please," Will whined, shaking his rump. Troy obliged him with three sharp smacks that were every bit as hard as Will liked them to be. Will yelled and raised his butt for each one, even though they left his skin bright, fiery red. Before the last slap finished ringing out, Troy thrust into Will's hole, giving them both the rough fucking they liked. Sex wasn't always this way, but when it was, they all revelled in it.

Will's ass gripped Troy's length, rippling around it as he sank in balls-deep. Troy loved watching his dick split Will open. He loved the drag against his cock when he pulled out almost completely. He loved everything about fucking Will, and—"Shit," he hissed. He loved being fucked, too, and Carlos' cock was thick, thick and long, and pushing through Troy's pucker. Troy didn't even think Carlos had his fingers all the way out when he'd started pushing in, because holy hell, that had been some burn, but Carlos was soon holding his hips, and that was good, so good.

It was perfect, better than perfect, if that was possible. Troy kept his hips pressed to Will's ass and he bent over him, the better to receive Carlos' cock. As soon as that thick shaft was so deep inside him Troy thought he could taste it, Troy swivelled his hips.

"Damn it," Carlos huffed. He tightened his grip on Troy, bruising him, marking him, and Troy shivered with the pleasure of being owned by these two men. He owned them just as much, and it was times like this that he knew it in every cell of his DNA.

Carlos thrust in even further and Troy gasped, pleasure shooting through his ass. Will moaned and dropped his head to the seat. His hand was still on his cock, and Troy had to brace himself because he knew it was going to get wild. He grabbed the headrest and got his other hand on to the floorboard just in time. Carlos pulled back, Troy following for a few inches, then Carlos slammed back into him, driving Troy's cock deep into Will's ass.

The truck rocked or the Earth moved, or maybe it was just Troy's head spinning. Whatever, he didn't have time to figure it out because Carlos set to fucking him like Carlos was starving for it. Probably was – they were all three kind of sluts for each other.

Troy lowered himself enough to drag his teeth over Will's nape. Will shrieked and followed that up with, "More!"

"Gonna give it to him," Carlos rasped, ploughing Troy harder.

Troy's teeth clacked together and he came up to his toes with the force of the fucking. He hammered into Will, each thrust pushing whimpers and curses from him. Troy arched his back, getting a deeper drive in, and Carlos cursed just before he laid a harsh slap to Troy's backside.

"Oh," Troy panted, his vision sparking with red and black spots. His balls drew right up, getting ready to shoot him into orbit. "God. Damn!" Whether he actually got the "Again" out, he couldn't say, but Carlos laid his hand down once more, the sound loud despite their panting.

Troy powered into Will's ass then like a madman, need ripping through him. Will's "Uhn uhn uhn," sounds were driving Troy insane, just like Carlos' harsh breaths and jabbing hip bones that would leave marks on Troy's butt. His hole burned and ached from the pounding, and his prostate was about too sensitive for much more. Carlos was nailing that gland consistently.

"Now," Carlos barked as he shoved in again. He punctuated the order with a pinch to Troy's hip, and that bite of pain gave Troy just what he needed to come.

Troy howled, his throat aching as he tensed from calves to neck, his cock throbbing. Will's ass clutched him almost too tight, milking his shaft in irregular constrictions. Will keened, and Troy was jostled by another hard thrust from Carlos. Then Carlos gave that rusty sound he made when he came, and hot cum warmed Troy's ass deep inside.

Will grunted when Troy collapsed on him. Troy would apologise later, when he could speak. He was doing well to just fucking breathe at this point.

Carlos' raspy breaths gave Troy a sense of joy, knowing he'd helped push Carlos to that point. Oh, he knew it wasn't just him. Carlos' cock might have been up his ass, but Will was just as integral to Carlos' pleasure as Troy was. The three of them made up a maybe unlikely partnership, but it worked for them, and damn it, they loved each other on top of it all.

"Gotta move," Carlos warned right before easing his softening dick from Troy's ass. "Get you two to the ranch, I'm gonna have to show you some more rope tricks."

Troy's already aching throat went dry at that promise. Carlos was the only man Troy had ever trusted enough to let tie him up. He was kind of becoming addicted to it.

"Need…to…breathe…" Will got out. Troy stood up, stumbling until Carlos caught him by the shoulders.

"Yeah, y'all make my legs shaky, too," Carlos said, and it was the easy way he admitted things like that that helped Troy. Carlos was a strong, tough cowboy, but he had no trouble admitting his needs, or the way his men affected him. That he didn't view those things as weaknesses assuaged Troy's fears about being a wuss when it came to falling in love.

"Make all of me boneless," Will mumbled, flopping onto his back and promptly sliding gracelessly to the floor board. "Ouch!" he said as he hit, his legs flying out and arms flailing.

Troy was still more fucked out than agile, but he lunged for Will at the same time Carlos did. Despite thumping into each other, they managed to keep Will from falling to his ass on the ground. Soon they were snickering, and Troy's heart hadn't felt so…so full, since they'd started their trek for the Mossy Glenn Ranch in Montana.

He was beginning to think they might just be able to make themselves a home here.

"That's the look I like to see on your face."

Troy glanced away from Will's brilliant smile and turned

to Carlos. "What look?"

Carlos' smile was a bare curve of lips, but it packed a sensual punch like you wouldn't believe. "That one, the happy, you-love-us look. Makes me feel like I could fly."

"It's an awesome look, Troy," Will affirmed. "If my ass didn't feel like I'd just had a huge dick shoved up it, I'd be on you like stripes on a tiger."

"Y'all know I love you both," Troy said more gruffly than he'd intended. "I'm just, you know, nervous about moving here and…and what my role is going to be. I don't know anything about ranching."

Will shrugged. "Yeah, me either, but I know Carlos, and I know you. The three of us can do whatever we need to, to make the Mossy Glenn a successful ranch again for our friends."

"And employers," Troy added. "Don't forget, Nick, Annabelle, and Rory are our bosses, too."

Will nodded. "Yup. So are their partners. We've got a shitload of bosses, so we are going to make sure we don't let 'em down. I'm sure there's plenty you and I can do while Carlos cowboys around."

Carlos snorted and started straightening his clothing. "Hand me the wipes out of the glove compartment, please."

Will got the wipes and handed some to Troy, too. "I have an idea," Will started, grinning fit to be tied when Carlos gave him an arch look. "What? It's a good idea! You know, we have to hire a whole new staff, or hands, or whatever you call them."

"Yeah," Carlos agreed. "Sure do since the place has been run into the ground and everyone fired or quit." He sighed and ran his fingers through his thick black and grey hair. "Gonna be a pain in the ass trying to find people willing to come back to the Mossy Glenn."

Will winked at Troy, then looked at Carlos. "So, what if we place some ads in some of the gay mags and newspapers?"

Carlos stopped mid-zip. Troy did, too. Troy frowned and cocked his head to one side as he contemplated the idea.

"You mean hire only gay cowboys?" Troy wasn't sure he was down with that. He trusted his men, but only a fool would want temptation right the fuck there with them.

Will shrugged. "Gay, bi, lesbian, trans—every colour of the rainbow, and straight, too, if they're friendly to us. Wouldn't think there'd be any bigots reading those kinds of papers and applying for jobs. Plus, I think they'd be more likely to understand what we have going on."

Troy sure felt like he'd paled, though he didn't know for certain. "I. Uh." He rubbed his forehead and finished dressing. Once he did so, he realised Will and Carlos were still waiting for him to speak. Troy grimaced and scratched his shorn head. "I hadn't thought about that," he said truthfully. "Just figured we'd be together and fuck it all, you know? I didn't even consider how other people would react."

Will nodded, but Carlos only grunted, watching Troy closely before speaking. "That gonna be a problem, other people's opinion of us?"

"You know it's not," Troy snapped, feeling peevish and petty because maybe it would be, a little, and he didn't want it to be an issue. He just needed to find his backbone. Other people's opinions really *didn't* matter, he was just being a worry wart. Troy shook himself internally and stood up a little straighter. "It's not," he reiterated. "But I think we should hire ugly men with shitty personalities."

Carlos' eyes widened and Will laughed like a loon. Troy raised his hands up, palms out in an almost pleading gesture. "What? I'm just suggesting we not be swayed by pretty faces."

And Carlos, who always seemed to know just when Troy was feeling insecure, pinned him in place with a dark stare. "You know you ain't gotta worry about neither one of us screwing around. You're all we want—me, Will, you. That's it, that's perfection."

If Carlos had said it in any other way besides his usual, calm manner, Troy's doubts might have lingered. But with Carlos so certain, and Will's heart in his eyes, Troy wondered why he'd ever doubted them in the first place. "Same goes," he said, a warm, comforting flow of love moving through him. "I'm okay with Will's idea."

Carlos didn't speak right away, instead kissing first Will, then Troy, thoroughly before stepping back. "We'll talk about it once we get to the ranch and see what's what there. May be we don't have any other choice. Montana ain't the most tolerant place for us folks."

"Neither is Texas," Troy pointed out. But they'd had quite a few friends, in the long run. Now they'd have just each other. Troy hoped it would be enough if things got nasty. "I'm not trying to be a jerk. I want this to work."

"This?" Will asked.

Troy resisted rolling his eyes, barely. "This, as in the ranching thing. I know we'll work. I just kinda worry." He tucked his hands into his front pockets and toed at the grass. "You know, like...like that news story about the gay couple whose barn and fields were set on fire? They lost everything except the ranch house. All their cattle and horses, and just 'cuz some dumbfuck bigots got a hateful hair up their ass. That's the kind of thing I'm worried about."

Carlos had his deep-thought expression in place, but Will was chattering almost instantly. "Yeah, well, we can put up security cameras and see, if we just hire people who definitely aren't bigots, they won't be likely to try to kill us. We don't have to flaunt anything, but I don't want us to discriminate against someone who might be more..." Will fluttered his hands in the air. "Stereotypical, I mean, yet still very capable of doing a good job."

"Let's not put the horse before the cart," Carlos finally said, drawing both of their attention. "We'll discuss this more, but right now I'd really just like to get to the ranch."

Chapter Two

"Uh." Will shifted in his seat and glanced at Carlos. "Did it…did it look this bad when you left?"

Carlos parked the truck by the first barn, shaking his head as he shut the truck off. "Hell no." It had been getting run down, sure, because Antonia, Nick's mother and Carlos' former boss at the Mossy Glenn, had blown every penny she could get her hands on—and not on purchases for the ranch. Or on paying the men.

The end result was, Carlos had been forced to sell off all the stock just to pay the men, and even then he'd been short because the bank had demanded money, along with a dozen-plus other creditors. And Antonia hadn't given a damn about anything other than buying herself more shoes. Carlos rubbed at his chest.

"You're thinking about that bitch," Will muttered. He touched Carlos' hand. "Those scratches have been healed up for a while. Guess the memory is still pretty fresh though."

Carlos nodded. "She was one vicious lady. More hate in her tiny body than in a convention of bigots."

Troy snorted and Will chuckled, but Carlos wasn't joking. "Neither of you ever met her. Trust me, I'm not exaggerating." He looked at the barn, amazed at how quickly it'd gone from looking decent to looking like it was about to topple into a heap. He hadn't left the Mossy Glenn very long ago, just a couple of months.

Wincing, he unbuckled his seatbelt and rubbed at his knees. It'd been a hell of a long drive from Texas to the Mossy Glenn in Montana, and he wasn't a young thing, that was for sure. Fucking on the side of the road hadn't helped his achy knees any, but no way in the world would Carlos have passed up that chance to be with his men.

"Let's start here and see how bad it is."

"Can't we check out the house first?" Will asked, and Carlos heard the exhaustion in the younger man's voice. Carlos looked at the barn, saw the graffiti someone had thought was worth driving out to the middle of Bumfuck, Montana, to spray all over the damn barn.

"Yeah, we can do that." Besides, Carlos was suddenly worried about the state he'd find the house in. Antonia had bought pretty things to put in it, but she'd broken a bunch of them in fits of rage. He wouldn't put it past her to have torched the house. "Hope it's still standing."

"After what we've heard about Antonia, I kind of wouldn't be surprised if it wasn't." Troy tapped his fingers on the dash, frowning intently. "She sure must be a whole different level of crazy."

"You have no idea," Carlos mumbled, relief making him almost dizzy as he pulled around a curve and caught sight of the big ranch house. "Whew."

"Maybe it's booby-trapped," Will said as he leant forward, almost touching his forehead to the windshield. "Like, in the Indiana Jones movies, we'll get out and step on the wrong piece of dirt, and arrows will shoot out after us..."

Troy snickered and started unbuckling his seatbelt. "You sure have quite an imagination, Will. Can't wait to see what you do with it the next time we're all fuckin'."

Just like that, Carlos' achy knees were forgotten. He felt flushed with the beginnings of arousal, and as he listened to Will and Troy banter sexual possibilities back and forth, that arousal grew stronger until his cock was half-hard. He kept his gaze on the house as they pulled up to it. The porch railing was broken in three places, and the screen door was flapping against the outside of the house, held in place by one hinge. Every one of the front windows was broken.

Will quit talking about sex long enough to exclaim, "Holy

shit, do you think she did this?"

Carlos shrugged. "Some of it, maybe. Not the graffiti." There was more of that horrible spray paint on the house. "That's got to be kids. Antonia wouldn't get her hands dirty with spray paint."

"Maybe she paid someone to do this," Troy suggested. He opened his door and got out. Will was right behind him, and Carlos got out as well.

"She didn't have any money left," Carlos explained. "Now, maybe this here's the work of some kids in the nearest town, or could be some of the cowhands she pissed off. There's a lot of that word," he pointed to 'bitch' sprayed on in bright red, "on the house. Some on the barn, too. I'm telling ya, she didn't make no friends here."

Carlos went back to the truck and took a camera out of the glove box. "Who's got the photography skills?"

"Will," Troy volunteered, pushing Will towards Carlos. "He's got to, being a private investigator and all. Bet he's had to snap thousands of pictures."

"Who says I do it well though?" Will took the camera then smirked at Troy. "But of course, I do. Because I am just awesome like that."

Carlos popped Will on the ass, getting a yelp from the man. "Well, get your awesome self to taking pictures of the damage, will ya? We need to send them to Nick and the others, let them decide if they want to spend the money to fix this place up still. They might just change their minds."

Troy walked over to stand beside Carlos as Will set about taking pictures. "We can fix most of this. I used to work for a glass company ages ago, right out of high school, did some carpentry, too."

Carlos looked at his lover and arched a brow at him. "You never mentioned that before."

Troy's cheeks turned dark as he blushed. "Didn't see any point to it. I've been a bartender for the last eleven years, and that's kind of all I think of myself as most of the time."

"You're more than that to me and Will." Carlos knew

Troy sometimes doubted himself, and that the man had a bundle of concerns about moving to a ranch in Montana, not the least of which was his usefulness here. Carlos knew Troy would fit right in once he got past being intimidated about learning new skills.

"I know I am," Troy said quietly, his eyes lighting up with his joy. "Wouldn't be here otherwise." Troy glanced around the yard, then turned and looked from the direction they'd come. "Those mountains still creep me out. Make me feel tiny, which is funny considering." He flexed his biceps.

"You are a big guy," Carlos agreed. "And I love that about you." He leaned in to whisper in Troy's ear. "Especially when you submit to me and let me have my way with you. Tie you up, beat that ass until it's red and you're begging me to fuck you. Oh yeah." His erection, which had faded, began plumping right back up. Troy gulped, his Adam's apple bobbing. Carlos palmed one of his ass cheeks and squeezed, hard. "Maybe I should take you out to the barn, bend you over a hay bale and—"

"And not without me," Will interrupted. Carlos looked at him just in time to get a face full of flash from the camera. "Whoops. Well at least it's already sunny out so you shouldn't be blinded."

Carlos rubbed at his eyes, seeing spots behind his lids regardless. "You know we wouldn't be fucking around without you."

"Well, duh," Will drawled, "I bring the fan- to the -fuckingtastic!"

Carlos felt a sharp stab in his head as he often did when Will created weird sayings. "All right then, let's get on inside, check the damage there. Then maybe I'll see about getting out my rope."

Will groaned and Carlos whacked him on the butt. Will could glare all he wanted, but Carlos knew how much the man liked getting his ass paddled.

"I'll go first," Troy offered, darting up the steps. Carlos was going to protest, since he had the keys, but then he saw the gap between the door and the frame. Someone had broken in already.

Troy pushed the door open and stuck his head inside. "Fuck, it stinks in here."

"Ain't no telling what's been done inside." Carlos caught a whiff of rancid odour. "Jesus, smells like a garbage dump in the Texas heat."

"No shit," Will said, elbowing his way past Carlos and Troy. "Well, there's garbage all over. Might explain the smell."

Carlos and Troy went on in and Carlos cursed when he saw all the trash strewn across the living room and entryway. "What the hell, looks like someone really did dump out a garbage truck here."

"Smells like it too," Troy agreed, fanning his face. "But I'm thinking rats and raccoons can make messes like this."

"Rats!" Will shrieked right before he turned and literally jumped on Troy. Lucky for him, Troy was quick and strong. He caught Will easily, hefting the slighter man's body up high. "I hate rats! Hate! Them!"

Carlos wasn't particularly fond of the critters himself. "Might not be the cause of the mess." Although he suspected Troy was right. Some of the mess might have been left by people, but there was that musky, fetid scent of animal faeces. "Take Will outside while I do a quick run-through of the place, since I know the layout of it." He tacked on that last part so neither of his lovers thought he was implying they weren't up to the task—even if Will clearly wasn't.

Carlos waited for them to clear out, making sure to get the camera from Will. It amazed him that, even with the windows busted out, the house still reeked.

Until he found the carcasses. "Aw, hell." Carlos had to swallow hard to keep from upchucking when he saw all the dead rats, and yes, there were some raccoons, too. His best guess was that they'd got into the poison in the pantry. It was supposed to be appetising, and it looked like it had worked.

Flies buzzed and he swatted at them as his stomach gurgled. He set the camera down and walked around dead critters and trash to get to the kitchen. With no electricity on, the refrigerator hadn't been running, and there was a good chunk of stink coming from it, too. Carlos pulled his bandana out of his back pocket and quickly tied it over the lower half of his face. He grabbed the trash can, trash bags, and gloves he found in the work tool drawer.

The camera he took back outside to Will and Troy. "Y'all go on and get pictures of the barns, will ya please? I'll handle this mess in here. If you see anything else—broken fences, down trees, stuff like that, snap a few shots too." He didn't bother sending Nick photos of the inside of the house. That was just too gross to do to someone.

Carlos got busy bagging up everything he could. He worked non-stop, not wanting Troy or Will to walk in and see any of the dead rodents. After an hour, he had all the bodies up, but there was still trash. That was okay, it wasn't as awful as what he'd already cleaned up.

What he was doing was the easy part. There'd have to be more hands hired to fix the barns and even though Troy was handy with carpentry, he couldn't do all the repairs himself. Not in time for the cattle the Mossy Glenn's owners would want to bring to the ranch. Will could help, too, but there was just too much work for the three of them.

Carlos piled the bags up on the back porch, which looked marginally less damaged than the front. He went about sweeping up the trash next, and by the time he had the second story done, too, a few hours had passed. He came down the stairs and veered for the front door upon hearing Troy and Will.

He saw them leaning against the truck, both men talking, sometimes at once, sometimes more politely. Troy was pointing with one hand and waving his other around like he was trying to encompass the whole state. Will was nodding and pointing here and there as well.

Carlos' heart filled with that warm, bubbly sensation

he knew was love. He'd never understand how he'd got so lucky, or what two young studs saw in a wrinkled old cowboy like himself. He was just damned glad they saw it.

"Y'all done with the picture-taking?" Carlos asked as he came outside.

Troy nodded and Will answered, "Yep. We found downed fencing, and followed it for a good while until we got worried about wolves and bears and animals that could make us their dinner." Will gestured at the house. "Is it safe in there yet?"

"Still need to bleach the place from top to bottom, and have the electric and water turned back on."

Troy snapped his fingers. "Shit! I was supposed to tell Nick when we got here. Let me text him real quick."

"It'll still be a day or two before it gets done. Will," Carlos waited for Will to come over to him. "Help me nail trash bags over the windows. Troy can figure out how to shut the door so nothing else gets inside."

"Okay."

Between Will, Troy and himself, it didn't take long to have the house closed up. "Guess we can either hit up a hotel or camp in a barn," Carlos offered.

Will harrumphed and cocked his hip. "Uh, like the barn has a nice hot shower? Man, I reek, and as much as I love you both, I'm not gonna lie. Y'all stink, too. Definitely vote for a hotel."

"Me too," Troy added. "We could all use a good scrub-down, and besides, I found this." Troy jogged to the truck and took a coiled length of rope from the truck bed. "That's your rope, Carlos. I dug it out from under the other crap we have here." Troy patted a vibrant orange and blue striped suitcase. "Will's bag was on it."

"I didn't want it blowing out," Will said, an impish grin on his face. "I *love* that rope."

"You're not the only one," Troy rumbled. He set his hot gaze on Carlos. "You have a promise to keep."

"I have several promises to keep," Carlos said, keeping

his voice deep and slow.

Will whimpered and pressed the heel of his hand to his dick. Troy just looked at him, desire tightening his features.

Carlos wanted to curse, because he wasn't going to be able to take them into the nearest town and fuck them senseless. Three men holing up wouldn't be tolerated in Ashville. Probably wouldn't be tolerated much of anywhere, but a bigger city was their best bet.

"Bozeman's a couple hours away," Carlos began, stopping when his lovers' expressions fell. He hoped he had a solution for that. "I've got in mind a long, hard night of fucking, so maybe you two hot-heads can fool around in the truck, put on a little show for me so neither of you go off at the first touch in the hotel room."

Will shook his head, but he was fighting back a smirk, Carlos could tell. "Carlos, our sexy cowboy, you ought to know that there's no such thing as a *little* show when it comes to me, and to that monster cock of Troy's." Will sidled up to him, eyes dancing with that mischievous light that Carlos adored. "And you know I can come again and again, like a never-ending fountain of spunk."

Carlos huffed out a laugh at that, because yeah, Will had the shortest recovery time of any man Carlos had ever known—and he could come five or six times a night, no problem. It was...awe-inspiring, really.

"Well then, why don't you two get on in, maybe get in the back seat so y'all can sprawl, let me see you take that big cock of Troy's so deep into your throat you can't taste or breathe nothing but him." Carlos' cock was going to fall off from being so fucking hard for so long. He might even end up having to stroke himself off while he was driving, then take his own sweet time tying up his men and marking their asses up. He could always let Troy fuck him, too. It'd been a while, and Carlos did love the way Troy's dick stretched him.

Carlos rubbed his hands together, eager to get moving. He got in the truck and noticed Will was already all over

Troy, biting, whining, pinching at his turgid nipples. They were a right fine sight to see, and Carlos just hoped he didn't wreck from being distracted while driving them to Bozeman.

Chapter Three

Will squirmed on the bed, the skin on his butt still flaming hot. He'd had both Carlos and Troy fuck him earlier—not at the same time, though Will was eager to do that, along with a few other things that would probably scare his lovers.

Or maybe not, because Carlos, despite his calm, cowboy appearance, is wicked-kinky. Thank God. Will had experienced more than one shock when Carlos did something, like insert a finger or two alongside his dick. Will shivered and bit back a moan at the delicious memory of that. Troy had licked him clean after, and that had made Will hard all over again. Insatiable definitely was his middle name, although it only applied to Troy and Carlos. Will wasn't stupid enough to risk the relationship he had with his men just 'cause something pretty or butch caught his eye.

And besides, he knew he could be a bit much to handle. He was damned lucky because he'd never expected to find one man to love him, much less two. Trying his best not to wake either of his lovers, Will eased off the bed. Usually he wound up in the middle of the love-pile, but this time he'd dozed off on the edge of the mattress. If his bladder hadn't been throbbing he'd have gone back to sleep, but now that he was awake…well, he was awake.

Will tiptoed to the bathroom and managed to take a leak without turning on the light. The hotel suite they had for the night was fairly decent, with a kitchen-living area sectioned off behind sliding doors. Will had winced at the beige, beige, beige colour scheme, but at least the place was clean. *And beige.*

A quick rinse of his hands and Will quietly made his way

into the living area where his laptop was. He'd set his bags on the couch because Troy and Carlos had been all over him as soon as the door closed. Will grinned and rubbed at his wrists. The rope had chafed him just enough to mark him. Troy would have matching bracelets left behind from Carlos tying him up as well.

They hadn't talked about anything other than what they were doing to each other, but Will's mind was percolating with ideas for the ranch. Granted, he had no experience with cattle or horses or whatever other livestock ranchers raised, but he did know people. His strength in this whole endeavour might just be in dealing with the people to be hired. He could run background checks on them, too, which would also be a good idea. Too bad he couldn't make a psych evaluation part of the application process. He'd had enough of dealing with nutjobs when he'd been a PI.

Granted, most of the real nutjobs had been his own family members since he worked for his father. Will shivered, glad to be away from him and the rest of his family. Being disowned was a blessing in his case. He'd been physically, mentally and verbally abused by everyone in his immediate family except his mother, who had long ago had her spirit broken. Really, if it weren't for Carlos and Troy, he'd be in a bad way right now.

Which was part of the reason he wanted to make the ranch successful. Troy would need some reassuring—okay, a lot of reassuring, probably—but Will knew he'd do everything he could to help, just as Will and Carlos would. Will could just picture Troy, shirtless, cowboy hat on his shaved head, swinging an axe or...or something that caused those big muscles to ripple and shine with sweat. He closed his eyes, the better to envision the scene.

A bead of it would trail right down the centre of Troy's back, following his spine to that lovely divot right above his crack. Will had traced that same path with his tongue numerous times. He knew just how it'd taste, the sounds Troy would make and the way he'd shiver before demanding that Will rim him. Carlos would be there too, forcing Will's hands behind his back so he only had his mouth, tongue and teeth to pleasure Troy with.

"I know that look. That's your horny-as-hell expression."

Will opened his eyes, startled at Troy's voice. He'd been so lost in his fantasy he hadn't heard Troy—or Carlos, who was standing right behind him—come into the room. "Uh." He couldn't be expected to think when all the blood had rushed to his dick.

"Yep, guess we didn't fuck him enough," Carlos drawled, and Will's entire body tingled with desire. Carlos narrowed his eyes and nodded. "I think he needs another round or two."

Will whimpered and had to tug on his balls to get some control over himself. Otherwise, he was in danger of spurting just from Carlos' rough voice alone. And while Will could recover quickly generally, he'd already come several times. Even he knew he had some limitations, and this erection he was sporting was liable to be it for a while.

"What are you doing up anyway?" Troy asked, crossing his arms over his broad chest.

Will gulped, because it sure sounded like Troy was a bit irked at him. That generally meant Will was in for some serious pleasure rather than anything bad.

"I had to pee."

Troy's eyebrows almost met above his nose when he frowned, and Carlos just watched him expectantly. Will gestured to his laptop bag. "Then I thought I'd do some research on where to place ads for the positions on the ranch. But I got distracted thinking about Troy shirtless and having you"—he tipped his chin towards Carlos—"holding my hands behind my back so I had to use only my mouth to rim Troy."

Troy closed his eyes and shuddered as he ran a hand down over his semi-erect cock. Carlos edged past him. Carlos' dick was huge, and even soft it had a heft to it that Will loved. He watched it sway as Carlos walked.

"Just how were you gonna rim him if he was only shirtless?"

Will jerked his gaze up to Carlos'. "It's a fantasy. His pants magically disappear." Will perked up even more when a better idea flashed through his mind. "Or, better yet, Troy, you're out there working wearing nothing but a cowboy hat, a tool belt and cowboy boots. Oh yeah." Will hummed and fisted his shaft, giving it a squeeze.

"God damn, Will's got a great idea," Carlos rumbled, glancing from Will to Troy. "I think that ought to be your uniform, Troy. Boots, belt and hat. If the other hands we hire don't like it, they can leave."

Troy came over and smoothed a hand down Carlos' back to the swell of his butt. "If I didn't know you were joking, I'd be nervous. Pretty sure you don't want everyone seeing me naked though."

Carlos' low growl caused Will's cock to shed a tear of pre-cum. He joined his men and cupped Carlos' other butt cheek. "I could just see both of you, naked, and Carlos, you would have Troy bent over the fence rail, fucking him with that huge cock of yours..."

"And you'd be doin' what?" Troy rasped, reaching for Will's shaft. "No, I know. You'd be on the other side of the fence, sucking me off."

Oh damn. Will was never going to get to his research at this rate, not that he minded. He'd find some time, somehow, because right now he needed Troy and Carlos all over again.

"I'm serious about trying to make the ranch a place that's safe for people like us," he informed them as he stroked each man from pecs to navel.

Carlos caught his hand and held it against his belly. "We know ya are. It's a good idea, if we can manage it."

That praise made Will's entire world a brighter place. He beamed at his men. "Really? I mean, I think we can manage it, I do. But you think it's a good idea? I figured with us living in the ranch house, even if we pretend to have separate rooms, the hands will figure it out, eventually. Or some of them will, and maybe they'll be more inclined not to freak out if they've got a safe place and all."

"See? That's a well-thought-out plan," Troy said. "Isn't it, Carlos?"

"You bet. I wasn't gonna hide our relationship anyway." Carlos gave them a serious look. "In case either of you had that in mind, we better discuss it right now."

Troy gnawed on his bottom lip and Will wanted to soothe his worries, but he also wanted Troy to just…have faith in them.

"We won't be running around flinging it in everyone's face, either," Carlos clarified, his voice a soothing murmur. "But if I want to hold your hand, or catch Will when he jumps on me"—Carlos winked at Will, shooting him a grin—"then I want to be free to do that. But I won't be maulin' y'all in front of anyone else."

Will bit back a quip about Carlos being no fun. Now wasn't the time for jokes, not with Troy still being so silent. Then Troy sighed, a gust of air leaving him that seemed to have sucked out all of his tension, judging by the way his shoulders slumped a little.

"I guess I didn't think that far ahead," Troy said once he quit chewing on his lip. "But yeah, I don't want to act like we're just business partners. I mean, I want to be professional, yeah, but I don't want any other guy thinking either of you could be theirs. I'd have to beat the hell out of them."

Carlos canted his head and grinned. "That'd sure make it hard to keep the hired help around. Plus there'd be lawsuits, and probably jail time."

Troy nodded. "Yeah, so you're right. It's best not to hide it, but not advertise it, either."

Will almost swooned with relief. "Well, now that that's decided, can we fuck?" He'd start researching tomorrow.

Carlos grabbed him and spun him around so quickly Will didn't even have time to squeak. "Aren't you sore?" Carlos asked while at the same time rubbing at Will's hole.

He was definitely tender, but not out of commission. "Not so much."

Carlos snorted then Will was turned again and hefted right onto Carlos' shoulder.

"Hey!" he exclaimed right before Troy smacked his butt. "Ow!" God, he hoped Troy would do that again.

By the time Will was plopped down onto the bed, his bottom was on fire from the spanks Troy had delivered, and his dick was so hard he couldn't see straight.

"Let me get a cloth," he heard Carlos say, then Troy was on the bed beside him, kissing Will like they'd been apart for months rather than asleep a few hours.

His ass cheeks were spread and a warm, wet cloth wiped him clean of the remains from their earlier loving. Then the bed dipped, and Troy sucked Will's lips hard at the same moment Will felt the swipe of Carlos' tongue over his hole.

Sounds he couldn't believe he made escaped Will as Troy began sucking up marks on his neck. His ass was thoroughly rimmed by Carlos, wet licks and nibbles driving Will mad. Then Carlos did the sucking thing too, except he sealed his lips around Will's pucker and Will screeched at the sensation, kicking his legs and trying to get himself fucked *right the hell now!*

He was pulled to the edge of the bed, his head supported by Troy's hands.

"Open up that pretty mouth of yours for my dick," Troy ordered. Will closed his eyes, not particularly comfortable in the position he was in. He got up on one hand and braced himself against Troy's hip with the other. Just as he opened his mouth, he felt Carlos move in behind him, nudging his legs farther apart.

Will opened easily, mouth and ass, eager for everything he could get. Carlos didn't hesitate, lining up his cock and shoving right in. Will gulped and moaned around the crown of Troy's shaft, then was promptly shoved forward by Carlos' thrust.

"Take it," Carlos said, or maybe it was Troy, Will wasn't sure anymore as he swallowed with Troy's thick cock in his throat.

"Aw, fuck!"

That he recognised as coming from Troy. Will pulled back, chasing Carlos' retreating cock as he did so, making sure to keep that monster in his ass. When Carlos thrust forward again, Will took in Troy to the root. Troy's curses were their own kind of poetry, odes to Will's and Carlos' sexual prowess—or at least their ability to bring Troy pleasure.

Troy framed Will's head with his hands and began to thrust, timing each one with Carlos' so that Will was getting both ends filled at the same time. His hole burned and ached and he knew he'd be feeling this round for a good twenty-four hours. Not that that would mean he wasn't able to play then. Nothing would stop Will when he was horny for his lovers.

Will slurped on Troy's cock and moaned and wiggled every time Carlos rammed deep into his ass. He curled his fingers into the sheets and arched his lower back, pushing his butt out, a silent plea for more.

Carlos did this snarling thing that always made Will shudder with need, and this time was no different. Then Carlos began fucking him harder, faster, deeper. Will could only hold on then, because Troy tightened his hold as well and began pumping in quick, shallow measures, not quite breaching Will's throat now.

Will was going to melt, or keel over from so much sensation. He thought that every time—that he couldn't possibly take any more, feel anymore, but his lovers always proved him wrong.

Will's own dick was leaking, the skin tight around his length because he was so hard. He needed to get off, needed it now! He mewled around the mouthful of cock he had, and like magic, there was a hand on his cock, stroking, tugging. Carlos', he realised dimly as ecstasy bolted up his dick. Will jerked like he'd been popped with a whip as he came, his orgasm firing right up his spine. He had just enough awareness to feel the throb of Troy's cock, then there was the burst of tangy spunk on his tongue.

Troy's shout was quickly followed by a low, long groan from Carlos as he pressed as deeply into Will's ass as he ever had. Will was filled top and bottom with cum, covered with it too as he'd splattered all over his chest.

Carlos ground against his butt as he pumped more seed into Will, and Will swallowed and swallowed Troy's load. Finally Troy kind of whined and Will opened his mouth, releasing Troy's cock. He peeked through narrowly slitted lids just in time to see Troy drop to his knees. Then he kissed Will fiercely as Carlos came down on top of him. Will felt Carlos' arms bracketing his and was grateful. He wasn't in any shape to support himself and Carlos both.

Troy ended the kiss with a sloppy lick over Will's lips. Will sighed contentedly, finally worn out in the way he needed to be. His research would definitely have to wait.

* * * *

He was still up before the others. Will made a pot of coffee, walking gingerly, wincing every other step or so. He'd have liked a shower, but that would have woken his lovers and they looked so sweet—not that he'd ever tell them that—curled up on the bed.

Will tapped his fingers on the counter as the coffee brewed. As soon as there was enough for him to pour a cup, he did, then he moaned at the first taste of the hot liquid. It wasn't anywhere near as good as sex, but it was still awesome.

He quickly drank the cup and poured another before making his way back to the living area. Once he had his laptop up and online, he began searching. First, he looked for likely online magazines to place their ads. He made a list of the ones he thought would suit them best. Next came the International Gay Rodeo Association—he figured surely some of the people affiliated with it would have some suggestions, maybe even know of people needing work. He fired off a few e-mails and was feeling rather pleased with himself by the time his rumbling stomach drove him back up off the couch.

When he peeked in on Troy and Carlos, they didn't look quite as cute, maybe because Will was on the verge of starving to death. Will watched them for a moment, but both men seemed really out of it.

Well, he knew how to wake them up. Will let out a whoop and ran for the bed, his sore butt only slowing him a little. He leapt just as Carlos and Troy opened their eyes, then it was a mass of tangled legs and arms and, Will was sorry to admit, his elbow making contact with Troy's groin.

"Sorry, sorry," Will said as Troy yelped and folded into a tight ball of agony. "Oh shit, I'm sorry! I'll make it better, let me see." Will tried to pull Troy out of his protective curve but he wasn't strong enough.

Carlos knelt on the bed beside Troy and put a hand on Will's shoulder. "How 'bout an ice pack, or something cold. Ice in a wet washcloth might help."

Will sprang off the bed and darted for the kitchen. He cursed up a storm when he realised there was no ice in the tiny freezer. Grabbing his key card, he hollered, "Be right back with ice!"

Except he realised when he skidded to a stop by the ice machine that he hadn't brought anything to carry ice back in.

"Well, fuck it." Will's pyjama bottoms had pockets. He put a couple of handfuls of the ice in them and headed back for the room at full speed. The ice was cold and way too close to his parts, but he figured he deserved it. He should have been more careful with his elbow.

The key card didn't work at first, and Will wanted to shout his frustration—until he realised he'd slid it through the wrong way. Turning the card over, he got the door unlocked and in seconds was back in the bedroom.

Troy was hunched over on the edge of the bed, Carlos

murmuring in his ear. Will kept right on going into the bathroom, where he found an ice bucket. *Why is there an ice bucket on the bathroom counter? Do people get nutted here regularly?*

Will put most of the ice in the bucket, but a few pieces he put in a washcloth. Closing the material, he turned the water on and ran the make-do ice pack under it. He barely squelched the water off it before turning the handle off and heading over to Troy. "Here. I really am sorry."

Troy looked up at him and smiled slightly. "Your exuberance is one of the things I love most about you."

"Oh. Oh damn it." Will handed over the ice and quickly swiped at his eyes. "That's so" —*sweet*— "kind, considering what happened."

Troy groaned as he placed the ice over his injured area. "Was all of us flopping, Will. Don't worry about it."

"Don't worry about it?" Will sputtered, flapping his hands at Troy. "You tell me sweet" —*whoops*— "shit like... like you did then I'm not supposed to feel horrible for possibly ruining your manhood?"

Troy turned a shade of green that was not the colour for him. "Ruined?"

"Manhood?" Carlos said at the same time. Troy and Carlos looked at each other. "Your dick and balls will recover, Troy, just keep the ice on 'em." Carlos turned his attention back to Will. "And you, manhood? Really? You been readin' some of those classic romances or somethin'?" He pointed at Will. "You're right, though. That was *sweet* of Troy, but it was also the truth. You weren't doing nothing except trying to play. It was an accident, so let's let it go."

Will looked at Troy. "Can I cuddle?" he asked hopefully.

Troy held one arm out and lay back on the bed. Will was beside him in a split-second. Carlos took up a position on Will's other side, nuzzling his face in Will's hair. "You know me and Troy love you something fierce."

"I do." Even though sometimes Will had to wonder why. "And I love you both, too, very much."

Chapter Four

"This isn't quite what I expected," Troy said more to himself than anyone else as he looked around Ashville's main drag. It was the closest town to the Mossy Glenn, and while it wasn't miniscule, it wasn't far off that, either. Tattered signs hung from worn posts, and he'd guess about half the stores had gone out of business.

Will grunted and stepped a foot away from Troy. "Small Town USA. I'm kinda scared."

"They ain't so bad here," Carlos informed them, "But I wouldn't go playing grab-ass in public, either. Just keep it cool and people will pretty much mind their own business."

Troy was sceptical about that and didn't hesitate to say so. "Small towns are usually full of big gossips."

Carlos hitched a shoulder up at the same time as he tugged the brim of his hat down further. "Yep, but there's gossip anywhere ya go, and generally people here get their jollies from talking, but they don't do no more than that. Least when I was living here it wasn't so bad, but…" Another shrug. "Guess I didn't pay much mind, either, and Nick wasn't out, so…"

So in other words, Carlos really didn't know if the townspeople were going to go all raging homophobic on their asses. "Gotcha. We can be cool." Troy cocked a brow at Will. "Can't we?"

Will rolled his eyes and huffed, then guffawed loud enough to scare the mules they'd seen miles back. Will did something, changing the way he stood so subtly, and yet that bit of flirty outrageousness was gone and in its place was a more masculine version of Troy and Carlos' lover.

Will reached down and scratched his nuts. "We gettin' supplies or standin' around oglin' the place?"

Troy goggled at him for a minute before snapping his mouth shut. Carlos thumped Will on the back of the head. "Maybe don't lay it on so thick," he advised.

Will spat a nasty-looking gob of God only knew what on the ground and Troy's stomach rolled threateningly.

"Okay, that's more than enough macho cowboy shit." Troy avoided the wet glob as he started walking. "What do we have to do first? Should we split up?"

In short order, Carlos had them each going about separate tasks. Troy's was to hit up the hardware store and get some paint and supplies for covering up the graffiti, as well as repairing the house. The electric and water were Will's task, as in setting up the accounts and handling the deposits. Nick and the other owners of the Mossy Glenn had set up an account for them over the Internet, so funds weren't an issue. Although they weren't anywhere near rich, the money was there for them to get things set up and moving.

Troy looked down towards the feed store where Carlos was supposed to be checking into stock and feed and things Troy would likely never have a clue about. Roger's Store was the name of the feed store, and it was easily the largest business on the main drag. Even so, there were only two vehicles parked in front of it. Troy wondered if it were in danger of closing, too. He felt an odd pang of sadness at the state of the whole town, which was odd as he'd never been a particularly sentimental person. It just seemed wrong that towns like Ashville were fading away.

Giving himself a shake, Troy headed for the ACE hardware store. He hadn't seen one of them in ages, he realised. Instead there were the big home supply places all over. Troy was kind of excited as he stepped into the hardware store. A young woman sat at a cash register between the door and the rows of merchandise. She perked up, sitting up straight and beaming at him as she raked him up and down with her gaze.

"Good morning, sir. May I help you with anything?"

Troy was too busy trying to peer at the goodies on the shelves to pay her more than a passing amount of attention. "No thanks," he muttered, really not far off from grunting his words as he made his way into the place.

There was a certain scent to hardware stores that had to fire up a guy's testosterone. Troy would bet his dick got bigger every foot he gained in there. He wanted to go check out the tools, the paint, the pipes, the lumber—he was in hog heaven, as his momma used to say.

A twinge of familiar pain accompanied Troy's thought of his mother. She'd passed away over a decade ago, and the loss was dulled, but still there. He wondered what she'd have thought of this place, this town—his relationship with his two lovers. Knowing his mother and her wicked sense of humour, she'd have cheered him on.

Shaking off potentially melancholy thoughts, Troy's perusal was halted by the emergence of a young man from a door labelled Employees. It wasn't the all-American good looks of the kid that caused him to stare, but the black eye and bruising down the side of his face—that and the big, guileless grin he wore despite what had to be a painful injury. Still, his baby blue eyes were lit with that rather mindless happiness of youth, the kind that always reminded Troy of an energetic puppy. Whatever had happened to him that caused that bruise would likely be forgotten in another day or two if it hadn't already been.

Blond hair styled in a hip yet conservative cut, and muscled just enough to be noticeable, the kid was something else. Troy would bet he was the quarterback of the high-school team, or maybe the rodeo team captain, or whatever damned sport they had out here in hicktown. *Straight as a board to boot, and he probably got the bruise in some dumbass attempt to prove how manly he is.* Troy should know, he'd done the same thing a time or three on his way to realising beating the shit out of someone didn't make him a man.

"Can I help you?" the kid asked in a voice that cracked

just once.

Troy glanced at his name tag. *Fred. Seems old-fashioned, and just right for this town. Jesus, what am I doing here again?* Troy snorted before he could stop himself and a flicker of irritation skittered over Fred's face before that smile was back, bright as before.

"I know, I look like a kid, but I'm twenty, and I grew up in this store helping my dad. I guarantee you there's not much I don't know, so give me a chance, why doncha?"

Troy scrubbed a hand down his face and tugged on his bottom lip. Fred tensed but kept that smile plastered on, and Troy nodded as he reached for the list he had in his back pocket. "Yeah, sorry about that. I was actually wondering what the hell I was doing in a town like this, not doubting your awesome sales skills." Troy tried a smile of his own and felt not nearly as cute wearing it as Fred looked. He'd have to bring Carlos and Will in here for some eye candy. They'd enjoy the view.

"Yeah, man, uh, sir. Sorry. It's just that I ask myself that same thing all the time. Thought I'd go off to college, you know, but family obligations and all." Fred shrugged and took the list from him. "Are you with those guys from the Mossy Glenn? Carlos, I remember him coming in here months ago for stuff, but that other guy, the little one, I hadn't seen him around before."

This time Troy meant to snort and he did so loudly. "That *little one* can take your ass out, kid, and he will if he hears you referring to him like you just did. His name is Will, and he might just be the one to teach you that you can't judge a man's strength by his size."

Fred looked sceptical as he darted a glance out of the large store window. Troy wondered if Will was out there, but was reluctant to check. Then he decided what the fuck, he had every right to admire his lover. He wasn't scared of some small-town kid with more brawn than brains.

Sure enough, Will was walking down the sidewalk on the other side of the street, chattering away at a woman. There was no telling who she was. Will could chat up a brick wall and get it to grin. She was flushed and fluttering her hands around, so he figured Will was laying on the flattery. Maybe he was hoping for a discount on something. He turned back to find Fred jerking his head down, like he'd been busted doing something wrong.

Troy frowned then a light went on in his head. His gaydar must have been rusty, and he of all people should have known better than to judge a guy by his appearance. It wasn't like Troy was the stereotype of a gay man so many ignorant people envisioned. Then again, he shouldn't be making the assumption that Freddy-boy was gay just because he'd caught the kid ogling Will. It was hard not to watch Will, no matter which sex you were attracted to. Will was so vivacious and active, almost vibrating with life, really. Who wasn't entranced by that kind of energy? It didn't help that Will was gorgeous as sin, with his high, sharp cheekbones and large hazel eyes. Almost ethereal, Troy always thought. Sometimes it amazed him that Will didn't turn to wispy vapour and slip right through his grasp.

"Will is..." Troy started, but stopped when he saw a burly man watching them with an air of open hostility about him. At least a decade older than Troy, he looked like someone had beaten him around the head and face with a big ol' ugly stick. Troy immediately felt like a jerk for the thought, but he could feel the animosity as the man glared at him with beady, heavy-lidded eyes.

Fred stopped pretending to read the list and pivoted to glance over his shoulder. "Hey, Dad, what's up?"

"That's what I'm a'wonderin'," the other man drawled.

Troy tried not to show his surprise. Yeah, Fred kind of resembled his dad in the height department, maybe even some in the musculature, but he wasn't carrying around his bodyweight in anger like his dad was. Troy had seen enough hateful fuckers in his lifetime to know one on sight.

Troy stood up a little straighter, letting his chest and

shoulders expand as he flexed. He wasn't delicate by any means, and he wasn't intimidated by some old bigot either. He'd also take his business elsewhere if he needed to. He arched a brow at the glaring fool, daring him to start trouble. Troy would sure enough finish it.

"He's got a list about a mile long, Dad," Fred said, sounding as chipper and happy as a blue bird singing a morning song. Troy couldn't detect a hint of falseness in Fred's tone either, and he didn't know what to make of that. Either the kid was just as bad as his old man, or he was dumber than a bag of rocks.

Fred ran his finger down the list. "You want to get started on the paint for the barns, or you want me to do it? He'll need a whole bunch of it to cover up all the graffiti someone did out there." Fred shot him a worried look. "Everybody in town was talking about it. Is Carlos going to file a report or whatever he has to do to find out who did it?"

Troy would bet every dollar he'd ever had that Fred knew who'd torn up the whole damned ranch, just like he'd bet most people in the town of Ashville knew, but they wouldn't be talking. Carlos thought the same thing, and hadn't seen any point in alienating the townsfolk by going after their kids. That'd probably just result in more vandalism.

"Nah, ain't any point to it," Troy answered, but he didn't explain any further. He did look the older fuckwad right in the eye, putting the force of his ire behind it. "I can take that list on over to Chesterfield if there's a problem here." Chesterfield was only thirty or so miles away, or he'd go to Bozeman, fuck it. They'd be staying the night there again anyway most likely.

Fred's frown deepened and he looked from Troy to his father then back again. "Why would there be a problem?"

Okay, the kid was dumber than a load of bricks. Troy didn't bat a lash as Fred's old man uncrossed his arms. That was when Troy saw it, the scraped knuckles on the asshole's hand. Those knuckles were raw, and Troy knew only too well how that translated—into the bruising on Fred's face.

Maybe the kid's not dumb after all. Maybe he's smart enough and a good enough actor to keep his emotions hidden. Troy had flunked drama in high school for a reason. He couldn't act his way out of a paper bag.

He waited, wanting to see how Fred's old man was going to play this. With those beefy arms uncrossed, Troy saw the name tag the man wore. *Fred. Of fucking course. Bet he calls his kid Junior.* Troy was just going to think of the father as Asshole Fred, or Asshole for short. He wanted to give the fucker a taste of his own medicine, but couldn't, and that frustrated him to no end.

"How long's that list?" Asshole asked, keeping his gaze locked on Troy.

Fred Jr swallowed loudly, obviously feeling the unease now as he read the list again, his lips moving slightly. "We maybe don't have everything he needs—" he began, only to flinch and let loose a muffled yelp when his father, surprisingly quick for his size and age, lunged forward and ripped the list out of his hand. Troy wasn't sure, but he suspected the fucker had got a jab in, too, because Fred sure seemed to want to grab at his side. Instead he fisted a hand at his hip and took a shaky breath.

"We got everything on here, boy, what's wrong with you?" Asshole snapped.

Troy had about had it with the whole situation. If he didn't suspect the kid would pay for it in bruises, he'd tell Asshole to fuck off and die. It took every ounce of his self-control to stand still and act like he wasn't ready to beat on the older man.

"I… I thought w-we were out of the h-hinges," Fred muttered, his breath still choppy. "We don't have those ones."

Asshole's expression darkened as he glared. "We got some just about the same that'll work. What's wrong with you, boy? Trying to run off customers when you know this economy's tearing this country apart! Goddamn liberals and—"

Though he cut off his rant there, the glare he sent Troy was laced with triumph, too. Asshole knew Troy wouldn't refuse to do business there when Fred would pay for it if he did. And Troy knew full well that 'faggots' or some other equally derogatory term had been about to follow the 'liberal' slam. Apparently the old fucker suspected that Troy had a limit, and tossing that word out would have been the last freaking straw.

"You always said don't discuss politics or religion with customers." Fred's voice quivered at first, but he sounded pretty damn sure of himself by the time he finished chiding his father. "It's bad for business, and you just said we needed his business."

"Get started on the list while I get the paint," Asshole snarled. Troy turned to see if Will was still outside, thinking he'd go join him because the hardware store had sure as shit lost its allure. The sidewalk was empty.

"Don't think you're gonna get away with talkin' like that to me, boy," he heard Asshole growl, meanness thick in every word.

Troy closed his eyes, still facing the window, and searched for a calm spot in his head.

"No, sir," Fred answered quietly.

Troy's fingers ached from the fists he'd curled them into, but he kept his mouth shut, listening as the other two men went off to gather the items on the list. He was torn between the need to help and the need to butt out. The last thing Carlos wanted was trouble here, and interfering in the fucked-up relationship between Fred and Asshole was sure to cause lots of it. Some people would say that Fred was an adult, and he chose to stay under his father's thumb, but Troy knew better. Family could fuck your head up like no one else, and once they did a number on you, you might never know you could be free.

Like Fred, who wondered why he didn't get to college. Shit. Troy wasn't going to be able to figure this out on his own. He opened his eyes and craned his neck, finally spotting Will, all smiles and laughter, chattering away to another woman. Troy needed that happiness more than he needed the air he breathed. There was just no point in existing without it.

"I'll be back in a couple of hours," he said to whoever the hell was listening, then he walked out of the hardware store and headed for Will.

Chapter Five

On the drive back to the Mossy G, Carlos listened to Troy describe the scene in the hardware store. Will was quiet, something kind of scary considering he almost never shut up. Carlos was afraid that hearing about the kid, Fred, and his possibly abusive father was bringing back memories of Will's own past from not too long ago. Will had been abused past childhood and into adulthood, conditioned to accept it as his due. Except Will wasn't tameable, and he had a spirit no one could break. Good thing, considering Carlos and Troy loved the ever-lovin' crap out of the guy.

"I don't remember having a problem with Fred Sr," Carlos said once Troy finished. "He wasn't the friendly sort, and I sure wouldn't have wanted him as a buddy, but he didn't give me any shit."

"Maybe he saw Troy talking to me or something, or just, you know." Will shrugged big enough that Carlos felt it against his side where Will sat between him and Troy. "I don't think I remembered my super-butch act the whole time I was in town." Will tilted his head up towards Carlos, worry creasing his brow with a fine line.

Carlos took one hand off the steering wheel long enough to rub at it. Will would shit bricks if he got a wrinkle there permanently. "It ain't your fault, Will. If that was the reason, you surely didn't turn Fred Sr into a bigot. He'd be that all on his own lack of merits."

"Yeah, maybe—" Will slapped a hand to his forehead and rolled his eyes up. "Was there a line, a wrinkle? *Was there?"* he demanded before Carlos could even answer. "Oh my God, tell me there wasn't. Lie to me, even. I'm not even thirty, I can't have wrinkles yet!"

"Carlos looks fucking sexy with his," Troy pointed out.

Carlos was damned glad he had thick skin and didn't delude himself about his looks. He was a cowboy who'd spent years, decades rather, working outside. Sunscreen wasn't an option if you wanted to remain in the closet, at least it hadn't been. He'd make it a requirement at the Mossy G, for liability reasons if nothing else.

"Well duh, of course he does! He's our sexy, studly cowboy. Makes me hard just looking at him."

"I'm sittin' right here," Carlos groused, even as his pecker began to firm up. "You ain't making it easy for me to drive, either."

Will squirmed, all eager, horny man, and ran a hand up Carlos' thigh before cupping his balls. "Oh, yeah."

Carlos grasped his hand and pulled it away. "Don't make me paddle your ass." Which, of course, Will wanted, and so did Carlos, but they liked to pretend otherwise sometimes. Or at least he did. Will was more direct, batting his eyelashes and wriggling excitedly.

"I thought you'd never offer."

Troy snorted and Carlos pinched Will's hip, giving him a little taste of pain to keep him happy. "Later, baby. Right now we were talking, and we got work to do at the ranch when we get there." He gave Will his full attention for a moment once he stopped the truck by the Mossy G's entrance gates. Carlos let every bit of heat and need show as he seared his gaze to Will's. "Once we're done with the chores for the day, then I'm gonna—" He stopped, grinning wickedly as Will whimpered. "Well, you know what? I think me and Troy will just surprise you."

"What!" Will yelped, his mouth flopping open and closed. "That's just evil, teasing me. You just wait—"

"No, you just wait," Troy interjected right before he cupped Will's chin and turned his face around for a scorching kiss. It was loud and sloppy and Carlos was going to be walking around with a hard-on for a while just from watching the two men kiss, but it was worth a bit of discomfort. Troy raised his head and looked almost as dazed as Will. "I promise it'll be worth it all."

"Always is," Will slurred.

Carlos was going to make it worthwhile for *both* of his men. Troy needed some rough lovin' too.

"So about this kid, what do you want to do?" Will asked minutes later when Carlos parked the truck.

"Don't know what we can do," Troy answered, echoing Carlos' thoughts. "I mean, the kid—Fred, he's an adult. We can't just report the abuse like we could for a minor, or if we do, nothing'll come of it."

"Troy's right. Fred would likely just tell anyone who asked that he tripped or something similar." Carlos tugged his cowboy hat down a little lower to keep the sun from blinding him, and because he knew Will was thinking about his own past and how Carlos and Troy had helped him get free of it, he offered a longer explanation. "It ain't the same as it was with you, 'cause we surely wanted you something fierce, and you were ready to ditch your family and their abuse. Fred might not be to that level yet, he might never get there, and we don't feel anything for him like we did, and do, for you. It's just...different."

Will made a grumbly sound and slammed the truck door harder than necessary. "You don't have to want to fuck him to help him."

"No, that's true enough." Carlos waited until Will glared at him. Sometimes Will liked to be stubborn just for the sake of it. He should know by now that neither Carlos nor Troy were the kind of assholes who'd let a person get hurt if they could help it. But the fact was, sometimes you couldn't help someone who didn't want it. "Can't make someone take help, either. Best we can do, I think, is make it so Fred Jr knows he's got somewhere to go if he needs it. Even doing that might turn his daddy into an enemy, but I'm willing to take that risk. We can shop elsewhere." The local hardware store wasn't as cheap on prices as one of the bigger retail home supply stores would be. "I'd like to keep most of our business going to the smaller shops, not the huge chain stores, but we'll do what we have to."

Will sucked on his bottom lip as Troy joined them, having got out of the truck and walked around to the driver's side. Carlos slipped an arm around Troy's waist and let his hand rest on the hard plane of Troy's rigid belly. The man was fucking built, that was all there was to it.

"If I can make a suggestion—and it's only a suggestion," Troy clarified, already holding a hand up like he knew Will was about to get pissed. He probably did, which meant Troy was going to say something sure to spark Will's temper. "I don't think you should go in there, Will."

"Why the fuck not?" Will snapped, and Carlos wanted to bend him over and fuck that anger right out of him. That would surely make them both feel happy and boneless, but now wasn't the time. Besides, he knew fucking wasn't the solution for every problem.

Troy edged closer to Will. Carlos kept his grip on his bigger lover, but his gaze on Will. Troy touched Will's chest, then rested his hand further up at the base of Will's neck. His voice was husky with desire when he spoke again. "Because, you fucking sexy stud, poor Fred had seen you before, at some point, and I'm thinking he wouldn't mind fucking your sweet ass a time or two."

Well, that yanked a growl right out of Carlos, the possessive streak flaring bright and hot in him. He barely kept from snarling threats of his own in regards to Fred Jr. Only knowing it would upset Will more kept Carlos' mouth shut.

Will's eyes lit with excitement, but not the sexual kind, or else Carlos didn't know what he might have done. But Will bounced up on his toes and started waving his hands in the air as he talked. "See? Then I *should* go in there and talk to him. He'd probably be more likely to listen to me—"

Carlos shook his head. "Not necessarily. If he's lusting after you or crushing on you, whatever you wanna call it, he'd be too nervous and horny to pay attention. And if he really is gay and his daddy beats him for it, you going in there might cause more pain than not to the kid."

Will's expression crumbled and he seemed to shrink into himself. "You think he got hit because of me?"

"No," Carlos barked at the same time Troy did. They looked at each other. Troy nodded at him, so Carlos went on as he gathered Will for a hug between him and Troy. "No way, baby. If he got hit because he got caught looking at you or something like that, then it's all on his daddy, ain't it? You didn't do anything wrong, and neither did Fred if he was looking." Carlos didn't like the young shit looking, but he couldn't blame him either. Will was damned sexy. "We're just guessing, anyway. Not a one of us knows for sure Fred's daddy is abusing him, and we sure don't know why he'd be doing it, either."

"Because he's an evil fucking asshole," Will grumbled, clinging to both him and Troy. "There's never an excuse for beating on your kid."

"Nope, there sure ain't." Carlos turned so that Will was truly pinned between him and Troy. He kept a hand on Will's waist and used his other to palm a handful of Troy's backside. Carlos squeezed it as he dipped his head for a kiss from Will. Will put more teeth than tongue into it, trying to goad him into that spanking and a fucking, but Carlos had already laid down the rules and he wasn't going to bend. They had work to do. "Later. You keep that up, and you'll be watching me tie Troy up and fuck him raw instead."

Will's eyes rounded and his dick felt like a fiery spike pressed against Carlos' leg, even through their jeans. Troy shuddered and exhaled gustily, his lips parting and glistening as if he'd been sucking on them. Oh yeah, both his men needed it, and he'd give them what they were wanting—but first he'd let it build.

"You could do us both," Will said, proving that he seemed to have an inside line to Carlos' dirty thoughts.

Carlos barely kept himself from grinning at Troy as

Troy's eyes went dark with need, his pupils expanding and chasing out the brown almost completely. Carlos ran his hand up to Troy's nape and he jerked the bigger man's head down. Will was going to get a little squished, but since Will enjoyed that kind of thing, it'd be all right.

Carlos pressed his mouth to Troy's almost violently. It hurt, but in that good way that made his balls tingle. Troy moaned and met him bite for bite and thrust for thrust, until finally Troy submitted and softened his mouth, opening wider and letting Carlos have at it. Carlos plunged his tongue in deeper, owning every inch of space he could reach. He felt a hand on his dick, palming him through his jeans, and knew Will was holding both of them in his hands. If he wasn't careful, Will would have him and Troy coming and that was not the way it was going down.

He sucked hard on Troy's tongue, felt him moan as much as heard it. Carlos eased back, but kept his hand on Troy's nape. "You think about that while you're working on those windows. Think about what I'm gonna do to you once we're done for the day."

"Oh, fuck," Will gasped, rubbing Carlos' and, no doubt, Troy's cocks. "Oh, oh, I'm gonna have to beat off or something, guys. You know I can come as many times as you want me to, so please, please let me—"

Carlos thought about saying no, but Will really did come quick and easy, and often. He just wasn't cruel enough to deny him such a pleasure. And he knew just how he wanted it to go down. Carlos made sure Troy held his gaze long enough to get the message—Carlos was going to make sure both of his men knew they were his tonight.

Troy gave a slight tilt of his head, and Carlos saw his Adam's apple bob. He liked Troy being a little nervous, and Troy needed it, needed to be pushed. Carlos squeezed his nape then stepped back. He took Will by the shoulders and spun him around, pressing him to Carlos' chest.

"Oh yes, yes, yes," Will started chanting, hips already undulating. Carlos looked Troy in the eyes and locked his arms around Will, pinning the man in place. He unfastened Will's pants and wasn't surprised to find him commando. Will was all about easy access.

"Get down on your knees and suck him," Carlos ordered.

Troy's nostrils flared and he tipped his head back, as if he wanted to challenge Carlos. That was all right if he did. Troy liked to pretend he hated being bossed around, but in truth he craved it even though he was afraid it made him weak.

Maybe he wasn't afraid so much anymore, Carlos thought. Troy dropped to his knees so quickly it made Carlos cringe and want to rub his own knees. He'd have had to kneel slowly or risk staying on the ground for a good while. Carlos shoved aside such musings and clasped Will's neck, right below his jaws. "You keep it down to moans and whimpers only. I don't want to hear a word from you since you're getting to get off and we ain't. You'll take what you're given."

Will bobbed his head, or tried to. A little pressure from Carlos where he held him at the neck, and Will stopped. He gave Carlos a very hopeful look, but Carlos wasn't ready to delve into breathplay yet. Will wasn't going to rush him on that, either. Carlos kept that hand right where he had it without altering the pressure. His other hand he kept clamped to Will's hip, restricting his ability to thrust.

"Take it all, Troy. Open that mouth up and suck his dick all the way in. Show me you want it." Carlos had to let go of Will's neck to hold him at the chest instead, and slide his other hand across Will's pelvis to keep him in place when Troy swallowed Will's long, thin cock.

Will's mouth opened as if he meant to shout, but all that came out was a strangled sound. His arms jerked, but since Carlos had them pinned at his sides, all Will could do was watch while Troy sucked him off.

"Squeeze his balls, Troy. Make him shoot in under a minute and I'll tie you up real good before I fuck you." They really had a lot to get done, but besides that, he loved watching Troy eagerly lick and suck Will's dick.

Troy's cheeks turned ruddy and he grunted as he hollowed his cheeks. Will moaned and jerked in Carlos' arms. Carlos caught at Will's hair with his teeth, tugging the silky strands hard once he had them firmly in his grip. Will keened and Troy pulled back, cum spilling from the corner of his mouth.

Shoulda told him not to spill a drop. Carlos released Will's hair. "Once you're done drinking him down, come up here and let Will lick your mouth clean." Then they really were going to get on with the chores.

Troy hummed and suckled Will's tip as Will kept up with the breathless sounds. Eventually Troy stood and attacked Will's mouth. He grabbed onto Carlos' hips, holding him with enough strength that Carlos figured he'd have bruises. That was fine with him, he didn't think he should ever be the only one leaving marks.

He almost had to separate Troy and Will, but eventually Troy stepped back and wiped his mouth.

"Now, you two ready to get to work?" Carlos asked.

"Am I ever?" Will retorted, but he fastened up his jeans once Carlos let go of him. "It's so much more fun to play, but yeah, get to bossing us around so we can get to the good part later."

Carlos swatted Will on the butt. "Yeah, so you grab the paint and rollers, I'll get the trays and ladders, and we'll get on painting the barns. Troy, you need help carrying anything to the house?"

Troy shook his head. "Nah, I got it. If I need anything, I'll holler."

"Good enough. How long you think it'll take you to get the place liveable?" Carlos grinned. "I can't fuck you and Will like I want to at a hotel." Then he narrowed his eyes and looked up at the bright blue sky. "Well, unless I gag you both so's you don't make too much noise." The idea certainly had merit, and making Will be quiet would be a challenge even with a gag on him.

"Uh."

Carlos tipped his head back down so he could eye Troy. "Yeah?"

Troy's cock was hard and pressing against his thigh, Carlos was proud to note.

"A gag?" Will squeaked.

"Yeah, why not?" Carlos would bet anything Will was already planning on what online store to shop at as soon as he got the chance.

"A couple of days," Troy rasped. "I'll make sure it's ready by then, at least habitable."

Carlos leaned in for a quick kiss from Troy, and took one from Will, too. "All right then, let's get this done so we can have us a real home of our own." Carlos really wanted that for them, and they all needed it. He hoped they could have it here, at the Mossy G.

Chapter Six

Considering he'd been tending bar for years, Troy wasn't too unhappy with his handyman skills. He'd got quite a bit done, and had only scraped his knuckles once or twice. At least he hadn't smashed his thumb or shot himself with the nail gun. All in all, he'd been damned productive.

Carlos and Will had got a lot of the painting done, too, although Will had sworn he was going to buy a paint sprayer in Bozeman tomorrow before they rode back out to the ranch. Troy couldn't blame him. Painting didn't seem to be one of Will's talents, or if it was, he must like to roll in the paint, too, because when Troy saw him walking up the drive, there was little of Will and his clothes that wasn't red.

Troy had a flash image of Will naked, rolling on a paint-soaked canvas, and his cock shot to full staff in seconds. He turned around and pushed against it, trying to ease some of the discomfort as his jeans pinched at that delicate skin even through his underwear.

"Got a problem there, sexy?" Will called out.

Troy scowled over his shoulder before giving up on getting his cock in a more comfortable position. He faced Will, and Carlos, who ambled behind at a slower pace. "I just was thinking how you'd look nekkid rolling in paint."

"Was already a damn near thing," Carlos hollered before Will could speak. "He fell on the paint tray. Twice."

Troy snickered and Will flipped him off. "Whatever. I still look fuckable and adorable." Then he turned and Troy just knew he was smirking. "And guess what, Carlos?"

"Oh, no you don't," Carlos mock-growled right before

Will shrieked and ran at him. Carlos sighed like his patience was being tested, but his open arms and soft smile belied that sound. He planted his feet shoulder-width apart just as Will launched himself in the air. "Oomph!"

Troy laughed, feeling light and happy inside as Will wound his arms and legs around Carlos. Their Will was a cuddler, and a tackler, and the combo was certainly entertaining, among other things.

Carlos caught Will easily enough, Carlos' long, lean body solid muscle. He cupped Will's ass and kneaded it as Will humped against him. "Enough of that, now," Carlos warned, right before he delivered what had to be a jarring smack to Will's butt. "Gonna make me paddle your ass before the drive to Bozeman—and I won't let you come this time."

Will groaned and dropped his head to Carlos' shoulder. "Aw, man. You know I can come again—"

"Not happening. You get spanked, you have to show enough restraint not to come or else there's no more fucking when we get back to the hotel."

Troy frowned and tried to calculate what Will's choice would be. Will leaned his head back and asked Carlos, "Why are you being mean to me?"

"I'm not being mean to you, just trying to give us all something more to look forward to." Carlos nipped at Will's neck and Troy found himself walking towards his lovers, need coiling in his groin. "And you love it when I tell you what to do."

"When you go all Dommy on me." Will did something that made Carlos rumble in approval. "I like it when you turn all big, bad Dom, cowboy. You know it."

Troy stopped beside them and saw the pleased expression Will wore. "You like him telling you that you won't get to come again or get fucked, too, don't you, baby?" As if he needed to ask. The answer was as plain as the smug look on Will's face.

"Well, duh. Boss me around and make me your bitch,"

Will proclaimed saucily. "I'll even dress up for you both."

Troy had to close his eyes and picture every gross thing he could to keep from begging Carlos to just let them play here. The promise of Will dressed up like he'd been over Halloween, wearing a short skirt and high heels, garters and thigh-highs… Even his makeup had been perfect. Troy had never been attracted to a woman a day in his life, but give him Will dressed in drag and he about lost his mind.

Carlos must have felt the same way too, because he got a look about him that made Troy and Will both shiver with anticipation. At least Troy was fairly sure Will was anticipating their fucking later, just like he was.

"You bring anything like that to wear for us?" Carlos asked in a voice more rough than not. "The heels, hose, makeup—all of it?"

Will smiled coyly and fluttered his lashes. "You have no idea how many sexy outfits I have to wear for you two. Just get me to a room and give me half an hour to get ready, and I'll make your heart stop."

"I'll be happy for you to make my dick so hard I can't walk," Carlos retorted. "I'd rather keep the ol' ticker going."

"Same here, except I'm already suffering with a possibly terminal hard-on." Troy tried again to adjust his junk. "Seriously, between the way it's getting pinched and the lack of blood to my brain, I can't last much longer."

Carlos guffawed and Will snickered. Carlos set Will down and immediately palmed Troy's cock. His eyes gleamed as he stroked and Troy tried to keep himself upright as pleasure rolled through him. God, but he wanted to lie down and let Carlos rub his belly…among other body parts.

"Maybe you need a little relief, hm?" Carlos mused as he kept up the firm massaging. "After all, you didn't get off earlier. You sucked Will until he shot, then you had to get to work. Doesn't quite seem fair."

Troy manfully bit back a whimper. Carlos was right, it didn't seem fair—but Carlos hadn't come yet, either. Then again, Carlos could fuck for hours before he came. Troy wasn't quite up to that level of control, and Will, well, he never would be.

Carlos leaned in and bit Troy's lip, the sting sharp and fresh and perfect. "Of course, I ain't all about being fair, not when it comes to something like this." He smiled evilly and stopped touching Troy. "So why don't you get in the truck? The sooner we get on the road, the sooner we can all have some fun."

"Jesus, you're cruel," Will muttered, but he was staring at Carlos with admiration and love in his eyes. "I adore you both, you know that, right?"

"Yup."

Troy had to clear his throat before he could manage to speak. "There's nothing I wouldn't do for either of you." *Nothing.* Because without them, *he* was nothing.

Carlos grabbed him and plundered his mouth in the way that always set Troy's dick to leaking. This time was no exception. He clawed at Carlos' shoulders, needing to mark the man just as Carlos had marked him inside. And outside, more than once. Fingerprints, hickies, the occasional swat to the butt, all had left colourful bruises on him courtesy of Carlos. Will, too, because he got off on leaving love bites all over Troy's body. Troy got off on it just as much as Will did.

Carlos pushed the heel of his hand against Troy's cock and Troy's world shrank down to the sensation boiling in his balls. He struggled to find a shred of control, but Carlos did his growling thing, the rough and low grind of his voice flowing into Troy's mouth at the same time he clamped a hand to Troy's ass.

Before he could stop himself, Troy thrust his hips. Fire shot up from his sac, his climax intense and sudden as it slammed through him. The first jet of spunk shot from his cock and Troy moaned, relief and ecstasy making him light-headed.

"Does he not get to come again tonight?" Will asked.

Carlos gentled his hold, and ended the kiss with a lick over Troy's lips that almost made him hard all over again.

He wore a satisfied look as he rubbed his thumb over Troy's bottom lip, and Troy was damned proud of himself for putting that look there.

"Nah, he deserved it, having sucked you off and not even asked for a blow job himself. Or even a hand job. Don't you think he had this one coming to him?"

Lord, but the tenderness in Carlos' voice was causing a flurry of jittery things to bounce around in Troy's stomach. Made him warm inside, too. He'd bet if someone could see his insides, they'd be all warm, velvety chocolate and unicorns, rainbows, puppies and kittens. Love had to look something like that.

"Yeah, he did."

Will sounded just as love-stupid as Troy felt. They were something, the three of them.

"And he gets to ride to Bozeman with cummy jeans on," Carlos said after a moment.

Troy groaned. "Swear to God, you just saying that made it all cold and nasty down there now."

Once they finished laughing and made sure everything was put away, they got in the truck, Troy offering to drive as he did just about every time. Carlos actually tossed him the keys, surprising him. "You haven't let me drive in a while. What's up?"

Carlos assisted Will into the truck, handling his pert ass quite a bit along the way. As soon as he was done groping Will, Carlos focused on him. "You ain't banned from driving or anything. I just needed time to get past the psychological scar from your last time doing it."

"You did scare the shit out of us," Will piped up from inside the truck, almost shouting to be heard. Troy opened the driver's door and Will toned it down—a fraction of a decibel. "I mean, you almost rolled the truck, and this thing is Carlos' baby."

"There was a deer!" Troy said, exasperation tingeing his voice. "If you two hadn't been all over each other, you'd have seen it." It'd been a baby, all tiny and skitter-legged.

Troy swerved, and narrowly missed it and its mama as she came leaping across the highway. If he'd have hit either of them, there was a good chance he'd have cried. *Especially that cute little baby. I'da been sobbing like a teenager at that damned vampire movie premiere.* "They were cute."

"That's your best defence?" Will asked sceptically. "Seriously? Aren't *we* cuter?"

Troy knew he ought to shut up, but damn it, he couldn't let Will get the last word. "Right now you're looking kinda obnoxious," he teased. Will stuck out his tongue and Troy got in the truck. "Nah, it was just an instinctive thing. I wouldn't put Bambi and his mama above y'all."

"I've swerved for a deer or two in my time," Carlos admitted. "Dogs and cats, too. Squirrels, well, I'd swear those fuckers are just suicidal. They always run out on the road then dive under your wheels at the last second."

Will snapped his seatbelt on as he agreed. "I know! I can't tell you how many squirrels I've taken out. And geez, I cried the first half-dozen times I offed one of them. Now I just puke. That *thud*..."

Troy shivered. That *thud* was pretty nasty. "I hate it when birds fly into whatever I'm driving. I've had them hit the side of the vehicle, but it's the windshield, oh man, that's just vile."

"Yeah, it is, and I think we can come up with more pleasant conversation for the ride to Bozeman."

There was something dark and dangerous in Carlos' voice, and Troy wasn't the only one to catch onto it. Will loosed a breathy little sound and Troy would just bet the man was a touch away from shooting his load.

"What'd you have in mind?" Troy scratched out, trying to fasten his own seatbelt while he felt clumsy with lust.

"Oh, I dunno. Maybe rearranging some of what we'd planned." Carlos reached over and pinched one of Troy's nipples and one of Will's, making them both curse. He didn't do it lightly at all. "I'm thinking Will's dressup is gonna have to wait. In fact, I'd rather he surprise us with that. Can't you picture us coming into the ranch house, finding ourselves greeted by Will dressed up for us? Man oh man, that makes me need."

"Yeah." Troy was going to have that image in his mind until it actually happened.

Will fairly bounced in his seat. "I could *so* do that! You guys are in for a real treat once we get settled in there."

"I know we are." Troy got the truck turned around and headed down the drive. He needed a change of subject, quick. Between the nasty mess in his britches and the potential for another erection if they kept talking about Will in drag, he'd be miserable all the way to Bozeman if he didn't get the guys to chatting about something else. "Did you get pics of Will in the paint?"

"Yup, sure enough did," Carlos said happily. "He camped it up, didn't you, Will?"

"Of course. I had to make sure I looked my best for you two." Will winked at Troy. "Especially since you didn't get to see it. God, I went down like Goliath must have when he got whacked in the head, just *wham!* Right off the ladder and into the paint tray. Yeah, twice." Will's laughter was almost musical, at least to Troy it was. It wrapped around him and spread the joy it carried right through him. "I was only on the first step though."

"And you wouldn't have tumbled the second time if you'd have wiped off properly," Carlos grumbled. "You just about scared a decade off my life, Will." His voice dropped into a deeper register. "I think you'll have to make that up to me."

Troy could well imagine the look Carlos was giving Will—that dark, commanding way he had of holding you in place with just his arresting stare. Troy couldn't risk glancing at his lovers when he was doing seventy down the road. If any deer decided to play dodge-truck tonight, it wouldn't bode well for the critters.

"I'll make it up to you," Will began. "I'll—"

"You'll nothing. Tonight I'll be calling the shots."

Well, damn. Troy clenched his ass, his hole aching for what Carlos was sure to give him. Or maybe not. Carlos liked to push him. Troy knew he might not get that big dick inside him at all. Even so, Carlos wouldn't leave him wanting. He'd drive Troy to the brink of pleasure and keep him there for a while before shoving him on over. It was an addictive experience.

"Okay, cowboy. I can't hardly wait, but meanwhile—" Will shifted beside him, elbowing him a couple of times on accident. If it'd been on purpose, Troy knew he'd have been hurting rather than just startled.

"What're you doing?"

Will held out his phone and waved it in front of himself. "Checking on the online ads I placed. I haven't looked since lunch time."

"Anyone contact you about them?" Troy frowned. "Where'd you place the ads?"

Will gave an exasperated huff. "I *told* you. The IGRA, Craigslist, a few other places. I hadn't gotten so much as a junk mail then but—Ah ha! Look!"

"Don't stick the phone in his face," Carlos said, just as Troy squinted to avoid being blinded by the phone's light. "And Craigslist? What's that?"

Will chortled and Troy tried not to glower as he answered Carlos' question. "It's an online want-ad like thing, and they have some personal ads up there that you wouldn't believe." Troy cut Will a seething look as Will went quiet. "You can find just about anyone to do anything with, or to. I'll show you when we get back to the hotel."

Why it was irking him so bad, Troy didn't know. He just hated the idea of Will scrolling through the pictures in the personals, the offers and come-ons. Hell, he didn't want Carlos doing it, either. He wouldn't mess with it himself, but he'd already promised to show Carlos.

"I didn't go into the personals. I wouldn't." And now Will sounded hurt, and Troy was a damned asshole. "Why would you think I would?"

"I don't," Troy gritted out, more mad at himself now than anything else. "I'm just—that site can—aw, hell." He swiped at his suddenly sweaty brow. "I don't know, okay? I'm not used to being jealous, but I guess that's what happened. I've seen the ads, some of the guys on there are hot as fuck, and the promises they make, just—damn."

"I gotta see this thing," Carlos muttered.

"I'll show you, but if you get mad, too, I'm going to hurt you both." Will sniffed and Troy jumped when he felt a hand on his arm. "I'm not going to hit you, although I was tempted to smack the bitchy right out of you. It hurts that you don't trust me, Troy."

Shit, he was going to ruin everything with his insecurities. Troy scraped some words past his tight throat. "I *do* trust you, Will." *Has Will looked at the personals? Is it cheating if he does? It feels like it would be, or something close to it.* "I just—" Telling Will he loved him so much he got all jealous sounded like something an abuser would say even in Troy's mind. He backtracked and tried again. "I never had people I loved and worried I could lose." Troy realised as soon as he said it that it wasn't the right thing, either, even if it was the truth.

"You're not gonna lose either one of us," Carlos said. "Won't happen."

Will was quiet though, and Troy glanced at him and found Will watching him intently. "I am sorry, Will. Carlos, too. I shouldn't be a doubter, or I should have more faith. What we have means everything to me, and the thought of losing it, well, I don't have the words to describe how that makes me feel." Solid black inside, cold to his soul, hopeless in a way that told him he didn't want to exist without his partners. *Terrified.*

"You can't let that control you, or hurt us." Will stroked his arm gently. "I don't know if you're subconsciously trying to brace for us ending, or if you're still adjusting to there being an 'us', but you have to have faith, trust, or else we can't make it, Troy. Love, loyalty, fidelity, belief in each other and our promises we've made. Those things are imperative in a relationship, but Troy..." Will leaned against him and began smattering kisses on his shoulder between words. "That will come with time. Just because me and Carlos dove in with open hearts doesn't mean you're wrong for hesitating every now and then. You'll get to where we are. You'll believe in your heart that we won't hurt you or leave you. Just trust yourself, love."

Was that it? He didn't trust himself? Troy had thought he was good with what they had going on, but occasionally he worried. Didn't everyone? But maybe he worried too much. He sucked on his bottom lip as he thought about it. Will kept on touching him, but he eased off on the lecturing, and Carlos didn't add to it, which surprised Troy. He listened to them discussing the responses to the ads Will had placed. After a while, Troy forgot to brood and started laughing along with his men at some of the replies.

"This one says he doesn't know anything about horses, cows, pigs, chickens or any other animals besides cats, but he sure knows how to ride a cowboy!" Will chortled and Carlos huffed out a raspy laugh. "I don't think he'll fit in for the cowhand positions, but maybe something else? Because I think a sense of humour is really important, too."

"Helps to have one out here," Carlos agreed. "Sometimes it's the only thing that gets you through a day. Unless you're me. Then it's you two that do it for me."

For a cowboy, Carlos sure could be smooth. *Must come from him soothing scared horses or something.*

"His resume looks good for anything but ranch work," Will mumbled. "Well, damn. I was thinking he'd be fun to have out here."

"Let me see it."

Troy figured Carlos meant the resume.

"He could probably cook for us, do the cleaning. We won't have time for much of that, and he would work cheap. Says here, room and board, minimum wage."

"Wonder why he wants away from—where's he from?" Troy couldn't remember if Will had mentioned it.

"Uh. How do I scroll here?" Carlos asked. Will moved and after a moment Carlos answered. "Oh, here it is. He's from some town in Florida that starts with an H. Not sure how it's pronounced, exactly."

"Florida, huh? Guess he doesn't like it there for whatever reason. Maybe he thinks a ranch full of gay cowboys will be nirvana."

Troy barely got the words out before they were all laughing. Why wouldn't their applicants think that?

"Maybe not just for men. We aren't going to discriminate, right?"

"Of course not," Carlos answered Will. "You got some women interested?"

"We sure do. Almost as many as we do men, I think. We've got a total of thirteen responses so far. Not everyone listed their gender, but most of them did. There's two with ambiguous names, but that shouldn't matter if they'll fit in at the Mossy G."

"Nope, shouldn't matter at all. Can you print those off so I can read them properly? Squinting's gonna give me a headache."

"We don't want that," Will purred at Carlos. "Got to have you in fucking form, right?"

"Right." Troy really, *really* wanted Carlos to fuck him until he couldn't walk, or better yet, couldn't think. He didn't want to dwell on how he'd almost caused a major mess with his doubts earlier. "I need you both," he admitted easily. Why had he let himself stress over those stupid ads?

"You got us both, and I'll make sure you know it well here shortly."

The promise in Carlos' voice sent a thrill through Troy. He signalled for the exit they needed and not another word was spoken between the three of them until they were in their hotel room.

"I got dibs on the first shower!" Will darted through the doorway only to squeak when Carlos caught him up short, pulling him by the shoulders back against Carlos' chest.

"I don't think so, Will." Carlos grasped the collar of Will's button-up and grinned as he yanked. Buttons shot out and Will yelped. "Get the rope, Troy. I got a good way to keep Will quiet." Carlos pulled Will's head up, pressing under his chin, and he devoured the smaller man's mouth. He let go long enough to rip Will's shirt off the rest of the way, then he was dragging his fingertips over Will's belly and chest, leaving trails of pink from the pressure.

Troy's cock throbbed, need tight and hot welling up. He turned and knelt beside the bed. Carlos had his work ropes, and he had his other ones. Softer, and in a variety of colours, girths and lengths, just looking at them never failed to make Troy horny. As he was already close to desperate, he panted as he ran the light blue length of rope through his hands. "Which one?"

"Which ones, you mean," Carlos corrected him. "That one in your hands to start. The black one, too. And your favourite, that yellow one."

Troy almost whimpered with gratitude. The yellow one was *his* rope. Carlos only ever tied him up with it. "Yes, Carlos. Please."

"I do like the way you ask so nicely. I think you even deserve a reward for that, don't you, Will?"

Troy turned around, ropes in hand, and struggled not to beg too much. "Please. I need, so bad."

Carlos pinched Will's tit ferociously, twisting the nub and getting a wince from Will even as Will thrust his hips. "Set the ropes at our feet and strip."

Troy hurried over to follow the command, uncaring that he crawled on hands and knees. He just needed to get to his men, and do what Carlos said immediately. Nothing else mattered.

Chapter Seven

Watching Troy submit was possibly the hottest thing ever, Will thought. Seeing that big, proud man on his hands and knees, crawling over to Carlos, giving up everything for them, that was just fucking arousing in a way nothing else could compete with.

Carlos pinched his nipple again. Will shot up on his toes, pain bright in his chest and his dick swelling with it all. He wanted to ask Carlos to do it again, but knew better. Carlos wasn't an ass, he didn't dismiss Will's or Troy's requests or needs, but this wasn't the time for Will to be putting his own body's wants first. Something was going on with Troy, and they needed to make sure he truly understood that he belonged to them and vice versa. Will trusted Carlos to get that point across, whether it was through fucking or talking or both.

Troy laid the ropes down to Will's right, his movements controlled and almost reverent. He sat up on his knees and pulled his shirt off, giving Will and Carlos a marvellous show of his chiselled torso.

Carlos bent, forcing Will to do the same, and he reached out to tug at one of Troy's nipples. "Get the other one," Carlos told him.

Will tweaked the other one before scraping a nail over it. Troy hissed and that big body shook.

"Aw, God," Troy panted, locking his hands behind his neck and pushing his chest out. His eyes were closed and his lips parted, a fine sheen of sweat glistened on his tanned skin. "Please, don't stop."

"Not planning on it, but you need to get naked, Troy."

Will wanted to get naked too. His pants were stiff with paint and his dick was achingly hard.

Carlos seemed aware of Will's discomfort, telling him, "You'll get your turn, but first, let's get these titties nice and red and sore."

Troy whimpered, a sound Will didn't hear from him often. It was like a jolt of Viagra to his system. His dick just couldn't get any harder.

"Stand up, Troy. I don't want to have to kneel until I'm fucking you."

"Fuck, I'm gonna end up coming just from listening to you two." Will pressed a hand to his groin, but Carlos caught his wrist and squeezed.

"No touching yourself. You either come when I'm fucking you, or you come just from listening to us, like you said."

Will canted his head to look at Carlos. "You're so mean. I love that about you."

Carlos kissed his nose then pushed at his shoulders. "You get down and get his boots and pants off. I've got something to take care of up here."

Will knelt and went to work on Troy's boots first. There'd been more than one time they'd forgotten, one or the other of them, and tripped over their own feet while trying to get their pants down. Troy was kind of wobbly, but a glance up assured Will that Carlos was keeping Troy upright. He had him by one nipple and one arm. Troy's chest was heaving, his breaths shaky, uneven. Will looked at the wet spots—the dried one and the wet one quickly spreading on top of it—and knew Troy was close. He got the boots and socks off, then went after Troy's jeans. The first thing he did when he had them open was pinch the tip of Troy's crown.

Troy shouted and Carlos made a disapproving sound. "Uh uh, you know we got to be quiet. You want a gag? 'Cause I can sure enough fix you up right quick."

Will waited until the first sound slipped out of Troy's mouth before licking the wetness from Troy's slit.

"Yes," Troy hissed, grabbing a handful of Will's hair.

"Aw, fuck yeah."

While he didn't raise his voice, there was a strident sound to it that made Will grin.

"Hold off sucking him just yet." Carlos brushed his fingers through part of Will's hair. "I think he needs something in his mouth to help him keep it down."

Will leant back, but Troy tugged him closer. Will turned his head and nuzzled the fuzzy spot where thigh and groin met. Troy wasn't one to wax or shave, at least not often and not his body. His head he kept smooth as silk.

Troy groaned as Carlos flicked his nipples, then he held onto Will's shoulders as Carlos walked off.

"He's just getting something for your mouth," Will said when Troy looked a little lost. "He'll be right back." He started sucking up a purple mark on Troy. There was going to be a neat line of them running around from groin to ass by the time Will got done with Troy tonight. If Carlos would let him do it.

Carlos came back and tied a rolled bandana around Troy's head. He'd fastened a ball of the material in the centre of the bandana, and that part he fixed in Troy's mouth. "Now, you want to scream, you just bite down and let it go into the gag, you got it?"

Troy's muffled assurance was quickly met with another round of Carlos working his tits over. "Suck his balls," Carlos told him.

Will left off the fourth mark he'd been raising up and went after Troy's balls. He pushed on Troy's thighs and Troy spread a little wider, allowing Will to get his head where he needed it for maximum nut suckage.

"Mmph," Troy grunted when Will took his big sac into his mouth. It was a stretch, but Will could do some amazing things with his big mouth.

Will couldn't pay attention to what Carlos was doing while he was sucking and tonguing Troy's nuts, but soon enough the sounds Troy was making even through the gag had Will whimpering too. He ran a hand up Carlos' leg, over to his thick cock burning hot through his jeans. Man, he wanted that thing in him, and he wanted to watch Carlos shove it into Troy until Troy screamed and shot his jizz all over the place—or all over Will's face. He'd like that a lot.

Carlos manoeuvred Troy onto the floor. "Will, go shower that paint off real quick. I was gonna have you wait, 'cause I like my men smelling like a hard day's work, but that paint might fuck up the carpet and there's no telling what the hotel would charge us."

Will hesitated, shifting his weight from knee to knee. "I don't want to miss anything."

Carlos gave him a piercing look. "It's gonna take me a while to truss Troy up right. You got time for the show."

Will sprang up and darted for the bathroom. He knew Carlos was right about the paint, but damn it all, he was horny!

"Don't touch your dick or ass except to wash them," Carlos said from the doorway, startling a shriek out of Will as he slapped a hand to his chest and spun around.

"Don't do that! I almost pissed myself," Will accused. "Jeez, Carlos. My heart's racing like crazy."

Carlos smirked at him and pointed towards his dick. "You won't be pissing out of that until it softens up some. Go on now, and sorry about scaring ya."

"You are not," Will groused, aware of Carlos' amusement.

"Nah, not really."

Will started the shower and got in before it warmed up. He bit his cheek to keep from yelling when the icy water hit his chest. It softened his cock enough that he had to jump out and pee, then he was back in and reaching for the crappy hotel soap.

As aroused as he was thinking about Carlos and Troy out there, Will still took his time, to an extent. He knew Carlos was going to be a while, and that the scene Will stepped out and into would be erotic as fuck. Sometimes Carlos would just lasso them and do a basic tie-up, but there were times where he showed his patience and skill by placing them in elaborate positions and tying them up beautifully. Will knew tonight was one of those times.

When he'd finished showering and brushing his teeth and hair, Will found Troy on his knees, his legs tied with the yellow rope binding his calves to his thighs. The rope had been run up his torso, where Carlos had done some fancy tying and bound Troy's arms up and behind his back. A red bandana was cradled in Troy's left hand. If he dropped it, everything would stop. It was the non-verbal safety measure they used when one of them was bound and gagged.

The rope was looped around Troy's chest in two different areas, then up again over each of his shoulders. It looked complicated, and hot, and Will reached for his dick before he thought about it.

"Ah ah," Carlos scolded. "You know what that gets you." He caressed Troy's flank and tipped his head towards the bed. "Get him that thin pillow, would you?"

Will got it and they slipped it beneath Troy's head and shoulders. Carlos palmed Will's balls then circled them with finger and thumb. He gave them a tug and Will's eyes widened and his knees went weak.

"You've been wanting something all day, haven't you?" Carlos said as he stood, towering over Will. "I know Troy likes to watch, and he can hold this position with his bindings for a little while, so let's give you what you want."

"What do I want?" Will asked, feeling his usual sass burble up. He arched his brows and Carlos and raked him with a look from head to toe. The man's cock had to be causing him pain, hard as it was. "You sure you know?"

Carlos' lips twitched and he held out a hand as he sat on the bed. "Yeah, and if I'm wrong, you'll surely tell me so."

"You got that right." Will had no problem speaking up about his wants and needs. He let Carlos put him over his lap, then wiggled until his dick was in just the right spot between Carlos' denim-clad thighs.

"You're gonna come from me paddling your ass, that and

what friction I let you have." Carlos emphasised his point by spreading his legs and taking away all that lovely, rough sensation from Will's dick. Will didn't get a word out before Carlos' landed a sharp blow on his left ass cheek. "Another nineteen and you'll be coming all over my jeans."

Will doubted he'd make it that long. Carlos pelted his buttocks and upper thighs. It hurt, but Will found that place inside himself where pleasure and pain mixed into the most amazing combination. There was nothing quite like it, and while Will didn't like to be hurt all the time, he did enjoy it when it was done right. Carlos always took care and never pushed too far. His hand was setting fire to Will's skin, and that fire was spreading through him, tugging his balls up tight as he neared his climax.

"Do it," Carlos ordered as his hand landed hard enough to knock Will's breath right out of him. The scrape of Carlos' rough jeans against his shaft combined with everything else sent Will spiralling into orgasm. He couldn't even yell as he was suffused with such intense feeling his body felt light with it.

"See, I told you I'd take care of you just fine. Now look there at Troy, his cock dripping from watching you…"

"Watching us," Will croaked. Troy had been turned on watching Carlos smack his ass and Will's reaction to it.

"But you're something to see when you come." Carlos rubbed his butt, kneading his cheeks, and Will almost whined as the heat flared out with each touch. "Now, you're gonna sit on your sore bottom and watch me fuck the cum right out of Troy, and if you make it through that without touching yourself, I'll fuck you afterwards, so get the wipes out."

Will knew Carlos meant what he'd said. Carlos could fuck for hours and hold back. Maybe it was an age thing, but Will doubted it. He thought Carlos just had that much control.

Will got the wipes out then sat with his back against the bed as Carlos stood, uncaring of the cum from Will's release on his jeans. All he bothered to do was free his cock, pushing his pants below his taut ass.

"Now, Troy's needing something rougher than he usually wants, aren't ya, baby?" Carlos asked in a soothing voice. "Nothing that'll make him really hurt, but just a harder ride than usual."

Such desperate sounds slipped from behind the gag. Troy was practically quivering from head to toe, and his muscular ass was flexing, as if begging for what Carlos had promised him.

Carlos picked up the lube and slathered some on his hand. He knelt behind Troy and rubbed his fingers down Troy's crease. "Hungry for it, baby?"

Troy tried to rock back, Will thought, but the position he'd been tied in didn't allow him such movement. Carlos smiled and put a hand on Troy's lower back. At the same time, he pushed two fingers into Troy's ass.

Will's spent dick reacted predictably, firming up with each stroke of Carlos' fingers in and out of Troy. By the time Carlos pulled off his belt and cinched it around Troy's waist, Will was dangerously close to not getting himself fucked. He shoved his hands behind his back and gripped each of his wrists to keep himself from grabbing his dick instead.

Then the beauty truly began, with Carlos rocking into Troy with small, steady movements. Once he was fully seated, Carlos leaned over and whispered that he was going to ride Troy like a bronc, and it was on. No more gentle, slow movements. Carlos shafted Troy like a man powerfully driven to do so. His hips slammed against Troy's ass repeatedly, pushing Troy forward only to be yanked back by Carlos' jerking on the belt. Carlos landed several slaps to Troy's ass, and gritted his teeth as Troy came.

The scent of Troy's cum was pungent in the room, and Will halfway thought he could have come from sniffing it.

"Come on over here," Carlos rasped, pulling out of Troy's hole. He pivoted enough to settle Will beside Troy. "I'll be right back after I wash off."

Carlos returned in moments, his cock wet from being washed. Will could even smell the soap he'd used when he walked past Will's head.

"Please hurry," Will begged, needing Carlos in him so badly he ached from it.

"I've got you," Carlos said. Will heard the click of the lube cap. Shortly thereafter, Carlos slipped a slick finger into his hole. "Hungry for it?"

"Yes," Will hissed, pushing out to take that digit in deeper.

Carlos did him one better, taking his finger out and pushing his dick into Will's ass. Carlos knew him well, and he gave Will that harsh edge he needed. His ass burned as he stretched around Carlos' cock, but Will shoved back, too, eager for the filling.

"Yeah, baby," Carlos murmured. He grabbed Will at the waist and shoulder and hammered into him. Will gasped and moaned, taking the pounding and knowing he was going to have rug burn all over the damn place when they were done.

"You're both mine," Carlos said, thrusting with enough force that Will's back bowed. "Just like I'm yours." He reached under Will and tugged on his shaft. Will opened his mouth to yell, but Carlos got a hand over his mouth. The thrill of that made Will's head spin as he came, and Carlos grunted, shoving in deep. He froze, spunk warming Will's inner walls as Carlos shot.

"Let me help you," Carlos said a minute or two later. "Come on, on your feet." Will swayed a little, but he managed to stand with an assist from Carlos. "Can you get the shower started?"

"Yeah." Will stumbled into the bathroom and turned the water on before going back to watch Carlos untie Troy. He sat on the floor and began to massage Troy's muscles as Carlos unwound the pretty yellow rope. Red lines marred Troy's skin and Will worked at chasing them out. Carlos joined him and soon Troy was moaning without the gag in place as he got two masseuses easing his stiffened muscles.

"Feel better?" Will asked Troy when they finished. He meant more than just physically, and the light in Troy's eyes acknowledged that fact.

"Yeah, I do. Thanks."

Carlos grumbled and stood, offering them each a hand. "No need to thank us. That's what we're here for, to love on each other, and love each other. Think the shower's still warm?"

Will grinned. "First one there's gonna get the hot water." He took off for the bathroom, ready to get his men into a different sort of playful mood.

Chapter Eight

Carlos surveyed the office. Like the rest of the house now, it was tidy and still smelt of fresh paint. The stark white walls were an improvement over the dingy yellow colour they'd been before. The furniture they'd had to buy wasn't the highest quality, but it was all decent enough. His desk was good-sized, made of pine, and it gleamed beautifully where the sunlight from the window landed on it. Eventually they probably ought to put up some pictures on the bare walls – paintings or photos, something – but for now, it was more than good enough. Different from when he'd worked here before for Antonia, the crazy old bat, but still familiar.

Will had worked hard on the house, cleaning and setting things up just so, while Troy had done most of the repairs. Carlos had spent his days working on the repairs to the ranch itself, mending fences and replacing rotted wood in the barns and out buildings, fixing up the corrals and such. He'd talked to Nick, one of the owners, and they'd set up a delivery of cattle and the horses Carlos thought they'd need. The ATVs should be delivered at any time, and they were ready to begin operations and make the Mossy G the successful ranch it'd once been.

It was a matter of pride for Carlos on one hand. He wanted this place to do better than it had when it'd been run by Nick's daddy, who'd been a bigoted, hateful man. It surely wasn't going to be hard to make the ranch more profitable than it'd been with Antonia at the helm. That woman had run the place into the ground.

"You about ready to start the interviews?"

Carlos glanced behind him at Will, who looked unaccountably nervous.

"What's wrong, baby?" Will was always up, mood-wise, with few exceptions. Now was apparently one of those times. Carlos pivoted and walked over to Will, catching those fidgeting hands in his own larger ones. Will's palms were a little rougher than usual, probably due to the cleaning and such he'd been doing, but they were still a hell of a lot smoother than Carlos' dry, callused hands. "What's going on?" There was too much worry bearing down on Will.

Will sucked on his lips for a second then released them, leaving them shiny with spit. Carlos fought back a groan, wanting to lick the shine right off them, but now wasn't the time for him to give in to his hormones. Will exhaled and looked down at their hands.

"I don't know. It just hit me, I guess. This is a lot of responsibility, running the ranch, making it work, hiring people." Will turned his eyes up to Carlos' then. "People's livelihoods are going to depend on us. There're three people already waiting in the front room, wanting jobs here. One of them was talking about her kid. We might have kids depending on us for food and shelter and—"

Will was awfully close to panicking. Carlos wasn't immune to the emotion himself, though it took more than the thought of those things to really strike it up in him. Right now those were thoughts he refused to entertain. And he knew the best way to calm Will down. Carlos tipped Will's chin up and kissed him, a hard press of lips and forceful thrust of tongue. Will moaned and clung to him. Carlos kept kissing him until Will went loose in his arms, the tension flowing right out of his body.

"We're gonna do okay, and we'll damn sure take care of our employees and their kids," Carlos promised him. "Ain't no-one going to be left high and dry even if the ranch does go under again. We'll make sure to keep a financial cushion set aside just for employees, okay?"

With that promise, Will seemed to light up. He sprang up on his toes and Carlos just barely had enough time to catch him. Will cuddled, that was a fact. Carlos held him and gave Will another kiss.

"I'll just get Troy then we can get started," Will said minutes later. "It's almost time for the interviews to start. Troy's looking over the applications and resumes again, but he doesn't need to. I think he's got everyone's information memorised by now."

Troy was trying his best to be useful, trying to prove himself, and Carlos knew that his and Will's reassurances helped, but wouldn't fix the problem. Troy was dealing with some insecurities that, in the end, he had to vanquish. Carlos and Will could and did love and support him, but there was only so much a person—or people—could do to help another person. Then it was up to the other person to do the rest. Carlos knew Troy would get there, but he sure wished he could just carry the burden for him instead. Then again, insecurity wasn't something Carlos felt too often.

"Go on and get him, and bring in whoever's first if you're ready."

"Oh, I'm *always* ready." Will turned and sashayed off, putting on a show that Carlos appreciated even if it did make him a bit stiff in the britches.

* * * *

Hours later, Carlos stood and stretched, his back and hips stiff from sitting too long.

"Hot damn, I can't wait to jump your bones," Will growled. "Too bad we have to hang around and wait for the other two interviews."

"We got time for lunch first." Carlos pushed his hat back and contemplated if their lunch time included a quick fuck or suck. *Probably not.* There was, however, time for some kissing. He gestured to Troy, who was watching him with a hungry expression. "Come here. You too," he told Will, then he had his arms full of hot, sexy men. They'd perfected the art of three-way kissing, although all of them liked getting sloppy with it too. Carlos let himself get lost in the feel and taste of his men, the scent and sounds of them until an unfamiliar voice startled them all.

"Uh. Holy shit."

Carlos didn't let go of Will and Troy. Whoever had talked had already seen them all going at it, so pretending otherwise was just stupid. He did ease them a little more to his sides, and they faced the short man standing in the doorway.

Short, and built like a fencepost, the man was thick, but not really fat. His eyes were huge, but that could have just been from finding them the way they'd been, all horny and happy at each other.

"Any particular reason you're standing in our house, uninvited?" Carlos asked in his deepest, meanest voice.

The little guy blanched, his olive tone turning to a rather unattractive shade of green. He looked like he wanted to bolt, and Carlos thought he would, right before the dude put his shoulders back and drew himself up to his full height of what had to be about five-three.

"Drake Cuttington, the next interview," Troy whispered right in his ear. "The ride-a-cowboy guy."

"Gotcha." And that certainly explained why the man was sporting a semi, Carlos couldn't help but note. Yeah, he'd been turned on by what he'd seen.

"My name's Drake Cuttington. I'm actually an hour and a half early, and I'm really sorry about that." Drake darted a look around before settling his gaze back on Carlos. "I, um. I have an interview, and I headed out early from the hotel just because, well, I didn't have anywhere else to be and I have a tendency to get lost even with GPS. Just so happens this time I didn't—get lost, I mean."

"Okay," Carlos said, figuring the guy wasn't done rambling yet. Drake proved him right.

"I was sitting in my car outside for a while, just waiting.

It looks bad to be too early, I know." Drake nodded, why, Carlos wasn't sure. "But I was afraid if I left, I'd get turned all around and lost, and the temperature gauge on the car was kind of high when I was driving up here, so I didn't want to push it, you know."

Will wiggled beside Carlos and Carlos remembered this was the guy Will thought would be fun to have around. At least he could tell a damned story, sort of. Will curled his fingers around one of Carlos' belt loops as he spoke. "That's understandable. It'd suck to get stranded between here and town, or wherever you might have gotten lost at, right? And Carlos, he's snarly, here"—Will jostled him slightly, but beamed up at him happily—"he's been misled by his GPS a time or two. That's how we all met, right, cowboy? Me, you, and Troy?"

Drake's cheeks turned ruddy as he listened. Carlos grunted. Will was just throwing it right out there, wasn't he? *And why not? Ain't like Drake didn't see us.* "Yeah, best damned day of my life." Carlos had no problem admitting it. He got kisses from both his men, though Troy wasn't quite as enthusiastic as Will, who probably left slobber all over Carlos' cheek.

"Yes." Drake coughed and shifted his feet, and Carlos saw that there was quite a bulge in the little guy's pants. Apparently not all things on Drake were height-proportionate. It looked like he packed twice the cock he should have for his size. Carlos pulled his gaze up and looked at Troy first. Troy arched a brow at him, but grinned, and Will snickered from the other side. Carlos' stomach rumbled and he put his attention back on Drake, who was eyeing him warily.

"Okay, here's the deal. You're the one whose resume has about every kind of job on it you can have without a college degree, right?" That sounded harsh, but Drake nodded and Troy moved away, coming back with Drake's resume. He read off from it.

"You've been a clerk at three different gas stations, and

quit each one because two of them got robbed, and the third one cut your hours." Troy ran his finger down the paper to the next job. "Lawnscaping."

Drake held up a hand. "I didn't scape anything. All I did was cut grass and weedeat, pick up trash and limbs. They wouldn't let me do anything else without a degree or certificate or whatever it was. Then I worked at a shoe store, but a customer complained because I wore heels one day." Drake glared at the paper, or perhaps at Troy, but Carlos was leaning towards it being the former and the memories it evoked. "Heels were allowed in the company dress code, and nowhere did it say men couldn't wear them, and I have fantastic legs. That firing was a load of crap."

"Some people just have no appreciation for the male form," Will huffed, posing with one leg out, toes pointed. "I have *amazing* legs."

Drake lowered his gaze. "I bet."

Carlos was kind of fascinated with the preening and air of competitiveness he felt sparking between Will and Drake. Maybe hiring the little guy would be more entertaining for him and Troy than for Will.

"Ahem." Troy cleared his throat. "Getting back on track, you've been a cashier, a cook at McDonald's, and again at La Cantera, a dishwasher, and an auto detailer." Troy lowered the resume and pinned Drake with an authoritative look. "What makes you think you have any skills we need?"

Drake gulped and his gaze darted all over the place. "I don't, but I'm desperate, and I'll do anything you need. Forget paying me, even, just room and board will do. And meals, I..." Drake blushed over every bit of exposed skin Carlos could see. It made his eyes seem a brighter green than they'd first appeared. He focused them on Carlos and there was a resignation in them that stirred up sympathy in Carlos. Not that Drake would want it. No one liked being pitied.

"I really *am* desperate," Drake whispered. "My ex—it was his house, his money, mostly. You've seen what jobs I can get."

Carlos was afraid Drake was about to beg, and none of them would handle that well. "Can you cook?" Will had suggested something like that when they'd discussed giving Drake an interview.

Drake nodded so hard Carlos was surprised he didn't snap his neck. "Yes, and not just fast-food stuff. My momma made sure all her boys knew how to cook, and cook well. That's part of how I helped out with the bills with—" Drake stopped and sucked in a sharp breath before continuing. "Anyway, I could do that, three meals a day, seven days a week—"

"Six." Carlos stopped him. "And on Saturday, you only do up breakfast. Sunday me or Will"—Carlos nudged him forward a little—"or Troy"—he tipped his head towards his other partner—"will handle our own meals, and we can sit down to lunch and work out the rest of the details. The hands have a kitchen in each of the bunkhouses, but you'll need to do up lunch Monday through Friday for them, and sometimes on the weekend when we're all having to work extra."

"I can do that," Drake said, and he grinned suddenly, his mouth wide and cheeks plumping up. "Thank you, all of you, and I don't gossip. I don't know if you all are planning on telling your employees about your, uh, relationship, or not, but either way, they won't find out about it from me. It's not my business."

Carlos canted his head and narrowed his eyes slightly. He wanted one thing very clear. "It *is* a relationship. As far as we're concerned, we are married to each other. Fuck the eyes of the law or anyone else who wants to judge, we love each other and are committed to each other, and while I ain't gonna run around telling everyone about it, I don't hide my men or my love for 'em, either."

Drake pressed a hand to his chest and his other to his neck. "That's just—that's, wow. Incredible, that you three found each other when most of us can't find one decent man." He sighed dramatically and fanned his face. "And yeah, oh my *God* is it hot knowing you three—"

"Probably you don't need to finish that sentence," Troy muttered, but he was looking amused by Drake's performance. "Think maybe you can get started on your job, oh, now? Or do you need a day or two?"

"Now's awesome!" Drake rubbed his hands together like a man with a plan. "I can't wait, I'm going right now. I saw the kitchen on the way in."

Carlos watched him head off. He looked at Troy and Will. "Huh. You really think he has nice legs?"

Troy coughed and Will smacked Carlos' arm hard enough to sting. Will glared at him. "Not as nice as mine, and it's a damn good thing I know you're teasing or else I'd really be mad."

Lunch was simple, sandwiches and mac and cheese, but it was nice to have it fixed for them. Carlos had Drake sit at the table and eat with them, and they worked out the finer points of Drake's job, including his salary and which room he'd be in after they all decided it'd be easier for Drake to bunk at the ranch house. Designed for ranch needs, the house had a small room built off the kitchen that had probably been used for other cooks. When Carlos had been working here before, there hadn't been the money to hire a cook.

The remaining interviews went well enough, with them deciding on hiring two of the three people immediately. Tomorrow there were more interviews, and Will had already pulled his ads because they'd got more applications than they could handle after a few days.

All in all, Carlos was pleased with the day and the way life was going for them. They'd soon have all the hands hired, and the livestock would be coming in. There was a chicken hut he wanted to fill, and if they got a few dogs and cats, the place really would feel like home. Carlos wanted that for himself and his partners more even than he wanted to make the ranch successful for Nick and his other bosses.

He'd do everything he could to see it so.

Chapter Nine

"Aw, hell." Troy joined Carlos on the porch, a cup of coffee in hand. "Seriously, who the fuck is doing this?" The first time the barns and bunkhouses had been graffiti'd again had been a shock, the second it'd been irritating. Now Troy wanted nothing more than to beat the ever-lovin' shit out of whoever kept doing it.

"Dunno." Carlos took a sip of his coffee and glowered as the ranch hands stood pointing at the buildings. "Fucker needs to cut it out. I'm goddamned tired of painting, and the sheriff out here's useless as teats on a boar hog. He ain't gonna do nothin' this time, either."

"Yup. At least it isn't a hate crime, I guess," Troy said, trying to find something positive about the whole thing. He'd expected to find slurs about them being gay but no, all there ever was, was awful spray-painted designs. "Whoever's doing it sure could use some art classes. He sucks. Or she, whatever. They, probably."

The screen door squeaked then slammed as Will joined them. He groaned. "Aw, come *on*! I don't want to paint anything other than my nails ever again!" He turned and pointed at Carlos. "Cameras—I told you after the last time we should get some. I'm going in and researching security cameras, finding out which ones are the best with our budget, then I'm ordering them from Amazon. They have every goddamned thing in the world on Amazon. I could probably buy an effective sheriff there while I'm online."

Rocky came over and stopped on the second step up. "This shit's gettin' old quick, bosses."

Troy liked Rocky a lot. With her hair cropped so short he

could see her scalp, and her stocky, thick build, she could intimidate most anyone who gave her lip—which she did, if any of the cowhands smarted off to her. For the most part, they didn't. So far their crew was coming together nicely and getting along well.

But Rocky was right. "Yeah, it is. I can't believe no one heard anything."

Rocky snorted and glared at the hands standing around. "A couple of those guys will fuck anything, which means there's some screwing goin' on every night." She shrugged. "I don't care, they don't put on a show for the rest of us, but it can get a little noisy at times. I'm bettin' it's the same in the other bunkhouse. People get horny, and there's those who're still treatin' parts of this job like it's a horny person's heaven, yanno?"

Carlos stiffened beside him and Troy laid a hand on his shoulder. So far, not a one of their employees had commented on their relationship, and Troy didn't want to repay that acceptance by delving into others' personal business. There was, however, a ranch to run.

"Are they fuckin' around on the job?" Troy asked, pressing his fingers against Carlos' arm. "We aren't paying anyone to get laid, so if that's the case, we need to know. They can fuck around all night unless it's a problem for others noise-wise, but during the day, they'd better be pulling their share."

Rocky hesitated for a second, but Troy didn't know if it was because she was watching the hands or debating whether or not to narc. He couldn't make her tell if she didn't want to. Finally she shrugged. "Nope, I've not heard anythin' about anyone messin' around on the job. Wanted to think on it first to make sure, but the guys I'm thinkin' of don't pair up on jobs during the day. Salt don't let 'em."

Saul 'Salt' Johnson turned and looked at them as if he'd heard his name spoken, which he couldn't have considering the distance between them and the cackling and bitching of the cowhands. Troy liked Salt. He was a little older than

Carlos, a little rougher and worn-looking. While he could hand out orders like it was nobody's business, Salt tended to be more of the smiling, easy-going type. The other workers found him an easy man to follow, which made life simpler for everyone on the ranch since Salt followed what orders he'd been given.

Carlos didn't look happy when he replied. "All right, but if that changes, let us know. We're gonna have to call the damned sheriff again and report this again. You and Salt get the hands divided up into who gets to paint and who's working elsewhere and get back with me."

"I almost think it's pointless to call the sheriff," Troy said as they walked inside. "I keep thinking the same thing I did when I stood in the hardware store. Everybody in Ashville likely knows who keep doing this, and I gotta wonder if it isn't someone who was pissed off at the previous owners. It started before we ever got here."

"Could be." Carlos frowned and rubbed his face with his hands. He pushed up too far and knocked his Stetson off, and Troy bent to scoop it up.

The black felt was worn and the hat blocked to perfection. Troy ran a finger around the thin leather band above the brim then he carefully put the hat back on Carlos, tilting it low in front.

There was that dangerous look he liked so much. Carlos was watching him intently, as if Carlos were a rattler waiting to strike the second Troy gave him a chance. Except it wasn't biting Carlos had in mind – at least not *just* biting. Troy touched the brim of the hat before trailing his fingers down the side of Carlos' face. He traced the sharp weathered cheek then thumbed the length of Carlos' jaw. Carlos' skin fascinated him. The darkly tanned parts of it and the paler lengths. Even those were darker than Troy or Will's suntanned skin. Troy loved every wrinkle and whisker, every single bit of Carlos, just as he loved Will.

"I like the way you're tender when you do that." Carlos placed his hand on Troy's chest, right over his heart, and Troy's pulse raced. Carlos' dark brown eyes were entrancing. Troy couldn't look away even if doing so would have saved the world. "You got such heart, Troy. Such a big, loving heart. You have no idea how much it means to me that you trust me and Will with it. We'd never break it." Carlos lowered his head, his lips brushing Troy's. "I love you."

They didn't say the words often enough, Troy decided as he opened for Carlos. He could hear those words every day, all day and never grow tired of them. Could say 'em, too, he thought as Carlos gripped his hips and pulled their groins together.

A second set of arms were around him shortly thereafter, Will pressing up against his back. Troy could feel the warmth of Will's moist breath below his shoulder blade, heating his skin through his shirt. There was no pressure for more, just the three of them locked into an embrace. Carlos nibbled down his jawline, and eventually Will was tugged between them. Troy and Carlos took turns kissing Will until he was a shivering puddle of need, then Troy had mercy on him and stroked him off with three quick tugs.

"Clean me up then go wipe yourself off." Troy held his hand up and hissed as Will licked the cum off his skin.

"Jesus." Carlos watched them and caught Will before he left for the bathroom. Carlos cupped the back of his head and whispered those same three words he'd told Troy. Will simpered and all but climbed up Carlos, mumbling "I love you" over and over.

Some days, even the bad shit couldn't make a dent in the good.

"The security cameras I ordered should be here by Monday," Will told them when he came back to join them. Troy put a finger over his lips as he spotted Carlos on the phone. "Sheriff?" Will mouthed around his finger.

Troy nodded and Will sucked his fingertip, giving Troy a devilish grin, then he let the digit pop out of his mouth. Troy would make sure Will paid for that little bit of tease later.

"I know you're a busy man," Carlos snapped, "I ain't asking you to come out here. We'll take pictures and write up what we see, and unless we find anything suspicious besides the graffiti, we'll just paint over it again." Carlos' features pinched up in a show of anger as he listened. He sounded ready to whale on the sheriff when he spoke again. "I'm only callin' 'cause I have to, in order to make sure there's a record of this happening again. I don't expect you to do jack shit about it." Carlos hung up the phone and rubbed the nape of his neck. "Jesus Christ, that man is an utter fool. Lazy, obnoxious son of a bitch."

Will murmured something sympathetic-sounding and hurried over to cuddle Carlos. Troy was thinking about the graffiti and the sheriff's unwillingness to do anything about it.

"You think it's someone related to him, maybe?" Troy asked, his thoughts spilling out his mouth. Carlos and Will looked at him like he was a little off, or they were a little confused. "The sheriff, I mean. He doesn't have any reason to be hating on us. He was a jackass from the get-go." The first time Sheriff Bowman had come around a week and a half ago, he'd had an attitude, and he'd eyed Troy and Carlos like they were idiots for calling him out.

"It's just some paint," Bowman had said. "Won't be any trouble to cover it up, and there isn't any evidence left for me to follow up on. Sorry, boys."

Carlos had just about had an aneurysm over the 'boys' part of that. He didn't like the term at all, and Troy had thought for a second that Carlos was going to rip the sheriff's head off.

"He just doesn't give a shit about this," Troy said, gesturing towards the barns. "He doesn't seem particularly hateful, just...like he doesn't care. Les would have a shit-fit if he heard about this."

"Les would beat some sense into the asshole," Carlos muttered. "Maybe we can get him to take some time off from policing in Texas so he can come up here to Montana and show the sheriff how a lawman ought to do his job."

"Les would sure as shit do it." Troy could just picture their friend Les explaining to Sheriff Bowman how to do his job. Les was huge, and serious as a heart attack. Troy had heard the guy'd never even smiled until a whirlwind of a man by the name of Adam had swept him off his feet. But Les was still a cop who didn't take shit from anyone.

"But he ain't here, and we get Sheriff Bowman." Carlos huffed then seemed to shake off his funk. "Well, regardless, we got barns to paint. I'll be glad when we can hire some more hands. Make this shit go quicker."

"I've got the other applications we never got to," Will offered.

Troy knew the answer before Carlos spoke.

Carlos shook his head. "Nope, no can do yet. We're budgeted for six, and we added a cook to that, so we won't be hiring more hands until we start generating some profits. At least, we won't be hiring any more full-time ones."

For some reason, Troy thought of Fred Jr at the hardware store. He hadn't seen the kid again—*no, he's an adult. I'm just old and think of everyone under twenty-five as a kid.* Troy had kind of hoped Fred would get out from under whatever hell he might be living in, but that was just it. He didn't know for sure that Fred was being abused. It was only a feeling in his gut, but he couldn't shake it. Yet for all he knew, Fred had already flown the coop and found a better life.

"We're gonna need more paint."

Damn, Troy would swear sometimes that Carlos knew what he was thinking. Troy cocked his head and tried to figure out if he was that transparent. "You want me to go get it?"

Will held up a hand, gesturing as he was wont to do. "Drake needed stuff from the store. I can go with Troy and get that, and Drake can help do whatever."

Troy tried his best not to smirk as he asked, "Afraid we got enough paint left for a few people to get started?"

Will snorted. "I know we do. There's a full can left from last time, and yeah, I am wussing out on the painting. I always get it all over myself."

"That's because you rush and don't wring the roller out enough. Slings paint all every which way," Troy told him for probably the tenth time.

Will's smile stretched wide and Troy knew Will was fixing to offer what he thought was a convincing argument. "Drake could probably do it waaaaaaaaay better than me."

That actually wasn't a bad argument at all. Troy glanced at Carlos, who gave the barest grin. "Yeah, you're probably right. Go square it away with Drake. We can't head out for an hour or so, though. Hardware store won't be open until eight-thirty."

Will squealed and clapped his hands. "Yay! That's fine, I can find a way to keep myself busy that isn't painting-related until we leave, like helping Drake get our breakfast fixed."

It was probably already done. Drake tended to get up earlier than any of them and have their morning meal waiting for them. Troy frowned. "I didn't see Drake in the kitchen."

Carlos frowned too. "He made coffee."

"No, I did that actually. Drake was on the phone and I told him I'd handle coffee duty while he dealt with whoever he was talking to." Now Will frowned as well. "He looked like he was teary-eyed, but I thought it was because he'd just woken up. That was a while ago. Weird that he hasn't come out of his room. I'd better go check on him."

"I'll start on breakfast," Troy offered, looking at Carlos. "Unless you need me to help you get the chores sorted out."

"I'm sure Salt and Rocky got 'em assigned to the right people." Carlos held up his cup. "I wouldn't mind some fresh, if it's not too troublesome."

"As if. We all need a truckload of coffee to get going." Troy took the cup. "I'll bring it out to you as soon as it's done."

In the kitchen, Troy heard occasional murmurs coming from Drake's room. He guessed whatever the call had been about, it'd been bad. At least he didn't hear any sobbing.

Troy got the coffee on then found some canned biscuits and a package of bacon. He got both on cookie sheets and put in the oven. He'd make eggs, too, but it wouldn't take long to scramble them. Anyone wanting over easy was up shit creek. Troy always broke the yolk no matter how hard he tried not to.

Outside, Carlos was consulting with Salt. Rocky had a paint roller in one hand and a thermos in the other. A horse nickered, cattle lowed, and a roster crowed. The ranch had got noisy in a good way pretty quickly. It was good, because Troy felt like they were closer every day to getting the ranch where they wanted it to be. Oh, he knew it'd take years to really have a firmly established business, but they'd get there, one day at a time.

"Coffee," he said when Carlos looked over at him. Troy handed him the cup and Carlos barely got out a thank you before he was chugging the steaming hot stuff. Troy left him to it and went back to finish breakfast. Will and Drake were in the kitchen, and Drake's eyes looked red and puffy. His face was blotchy, and his hands shook as he pulled the cookie sheets out of the oven. "Want me to get those?"

"I got it," Drake rasped.

Will shrugged and made shooing motions with his hands. "Go back outside and let Carlos know grub's on, please?"

Troy traipsed back out and met Carlos on the porch. "It's ready."

Breakfast was weird, only because Troy knew they were all worried about Drake. By the time he and Will got on the road to Ashville, Troy was brimming with curiosity.

Will didn't keep him waiting. "I don't know what was said, but that was apparently Drake's ex on the phone earlier."

"Is Drake going to leave us and go back to him?" Was he awful for worrying about who'd be doing the cooking first and foremost? *Yeah, probably.*

"I don't think so. Drake was pretty mad, and maybe scared. I couldn't tell for sure since he wouldn't talk about it, but I *think* it was fear I saw a time or two in his expression." Will let out a wispy whistle. "Man, I have to wonder about that."

"What do you mean?"

Will leaned against the door and looked at him. "I mean, if he was afraid, why? Is his ex a psycho-stalker? Or did he maybe expose Drake to something?"

"Like HIV?" Troy didn't like saying it, but avoiding one of the realities of life was just plain dumb, and he wasn't a complete idiot. "Is that what you mean?"

Will rolled his head and looked out of the window. "Probably I'm just being melodramatic, and misreading everything. I shouldn't have said anything, I guess, but it's worrying me and telling you and Carlos, that's the only way I can keep it from knotting up inside and driving me nuts."

Troy understood that, he certainly did. "Of course you should tell us. It isn't like we're going to go spreading gossip. You're worried, and we're here for you. Besides, I think maybe you're on to something. Drake likes you, y'all get along good. If you can, find a way to get him to talk to you some more, or just, I don't know, offer to drive him to the clinic in Bozeman for testing."

"They have at-home test kits now."

"I read about that." Troy glanced at Will, relieved to see him less stressed-looking. "Not sure how they work, mainly because I heard of them after we all got tested and ditched the rubbers. Guess I should stay informed in case anyone else needs advice, huh?" His mind shot to Fred Jr. Troy wasn't attracted to the other man in the least, but he couldn't seem to stop worrying over him.

"He reminds you of me, I bet."

Troy almost jerked the wheel, he was so startled. "How the hell do you and Carlos *do* that?"

"Do what?"

Oh, he'd just bet Will had on his most innocent expression. Troy wasn't going to check.

"How do y'all know what I'm thinking half the time?"

Will chuckled. "Oh, that. It's because we know you, we love you, and you're actually really transparent now that you've opened up to us. Plus, you're not the only one. When you told us about Fred, I figured he'd remind you both of me and the situation I'd been in. It's been hell keeping myself from going and checking on him. Although I have called the store on occasion."

Troy pulled the truck to the side of the road. He had to, because damn it, he needed to look at Will as they talked about this. "Why did you do that?"

Will hitched up a shoulder. "Well, because I was worried, and I knew you and Carlos were. Carlos is more focused on us, but don't think he hasn't wondered about Fred. So I'd block my number from showing every few days, and call the store. If Fred Jr answered, I'd ask for the price for some item or another. If the old fucker answered, I just hung up." Will pursed his lips. "Okay, once I started chattering about goats and flowers, but other than that, I just hung up on the jerk."

"What'd he do then?"

"He called me a stupid asshole. Not very creative, and definitely no fun."

"You're something else, you know it?" Troy was always astounded by how lucky he was to have two awesome, intelligent partners. "I didn't even think of checking up on him that way. When was the last time you called?"

Will held up his phone. "How about now?" The ringing was loud, letting Troy know Will had the speaker on. After the second ring, the phone was answered. Troy recognised Fred Jr's voice and was relieved that he wasn't dead. Will chattered about needing to find out what was wrong with his toilet, and Troy got the truck back on the road.

In town, he parked at the grocers. "I'll walk to the

hardware store and leave the truck here in case you get done before I do. Don't want you to have to lug around bags of shit."

Will grimaced. "Well, duh. That'd be disgusting. Why would anyone tote around bags of shit? Unless they had some weird fetish maybe."

"For gardening," Troy couldn't help but point out. "And you know that wasn't what I meant."

Will winked and took off for the store. Troy strolled down the sidewalk, enjoying the cold, brisk morning air and the bright sunlight. He'd loved Texas, even with its fucked-up politics, but Troy would swear the air in Montana was purer. At least it seemed so in the part of Montana he now lived in.

The hardware store actually seemed to be hopping, with several customers inside. Troy thought one or two of them sent him looks bordering on hostile, but his size was such that he doubted anyone would really mess with him. Whether it was because he was new in town or because people had somehow figured out he was gay, Troy didn't particularly give a damn.

He reckoned the gossips had heard about the ads Will had placed. Things like that always got around, and since some of their employees had stayed at the hotel in Ashville when they came for the interview. There was no telling who'd said what to whom. Thinking about it, that could possibly explain the sheriff's problem after all. Troy wanted to smack himself for not realising that sooner. But, he wouldn't bring it up, because Will might feel like he'd put them at risk, and that just wasn't so. People were just mean as hell sometimes.

A guy Troy hadn't seen there before was behind the paint counter, mixing up some colour for a woman who looked like she needed some more coffee. Her hair was standing every which way and she kept yawning big enough she could have caught a good-sized bass with her mouth.

After he handed the paint to her, the employee turned to

him. Dirty blond hair and brown eyes, and a face just shy of handsome, the guy shot Troy a smile.

Troy glanced at his tag. "Morning, Hank. Can I get six gallons of Barn Red, exterior, of course?"

"I can sure enough do that, man. You want to look around while I get it mixed for you?"

"Yeah." Like Troy needed to be asked. He wandered down the closest aisle, checking out a thing or two. He didn't see Fred Jr anywhere, but that didn't mean anything since Will had just been on the phone with him not half an hour before. Three aisles over, he heard a customer ask, "Where's that boy of yours, Fred? He was in here earlier and I'm tired of waiting around for help."

"He's not feeling so good. You'll have to wait or come back later. I can get your order together if you want to leave a list, Greg."

Anger coursed through Troy. What had happened in the short period of time since Will had called the hardware store? Troy thought it over, and remembered Will laughing and cracking a joke or two. Fred Jr had laughed, too. Was that what had caused a problem? Troy was getting a headache trying to figure out what was going on. For all he knew, Fred Jr really was sick. Will could make just about anyone laugh, and he was cheery enough that it would rub off on you. He shouldn't be assuming anything when he'd heard Fred's dad say he was sick.

And yet Troy turned and started edging towards the back of the store. The restrooms were there, and right past them was that doorway Fred Sr had come out of last time Troy had been there. It was a different door than the one leading out to the lumber yard, so Troy was hoping it was an office or storage room. Somewhere that a sick employee would camp out in.

Careful to keep from drawing attention to himself, Troy moseyed along looking at things. Sneaking had seemed a good plan at first, but that was suspicious as hell and would surely be noticed. A guy looking at tools, hell, even his haters couldn't make anything out of that. Just like they couldn't say a thing if he had to take a piss.

Troy made sure to keep his steps steady and his posture casual as he walked to the restrooms. One man in particular glared at him as if he'd like nothing better than to skin Troy alive. Troy paused and levelled his own look at the man, who scowled and mouthed 'faggot' at him before scampering off like a mangy rodent.

Troy's hands ached from curling them into fists. He wanted to chase the man and beat the hate out of him, but he'd have a better chance of killing him first. That wasn't the person Troy was, nor wanted to be. He resumed his trek to the restrooms.

The men's room was clean if a bit worn. One of the faucets dripped, a fact that irked the shit out of Troy. It was just wrong for that to be going on in a hardware store. He drained his bladder and washed his hands, relieved not to have encountered anyone else in the restroom. He supposed none of the men were brave enough to go in there with a gay man for fear Troy would be overcome by lust and have to fuck their irresistible fat asses.

"So many misconceptions, so little time to correct them," Troy whispered to himself. He checked and saw that no one was looking his way. Troy slid around the corner to the swinging doors and pushed one open slowly, afraid it'd make some noise. As soon as he got it open enough, he slipped inside and eased it shut.

The room was dark, but not pitch. He blinked a few times and spotted Fred Jr sitting hunched over on a box. Troy approached him slowly and noted that Fred was cradling his arm, or his ribs, it was hard to tell. He let his foot drag, not wanting to startle the kid.

"Hey, you okay there?" he asked when he got close enough that he thought Fred could hear his whisper.

Fred didn't answer him. Troy asked again, and when he still didn't get a reply, he touched Fred's shoulder. Fred didn't move. Fear shot through Troy and he fished his phone out of his pocket. Keeping his tone calm and his voice low, he tried again. "Hey, hey, kid, you okay?"

Troy moved his fingers over until he felt Fred's pulse, faint and not really steady. "Fuck!" Troy unlocked his phone and dialled for emergency services as he tried to get his hand under Fred's arm. The kid was sitting with one knee up, his back to the wall, and an arm around his knee with his other arm around his middle. Troy felt a bare puff of breath leave Fred's lips just as the emergency dispatch operator answered. Troy didn't even know if there was an ambulance service or a hospital in Ashville, but he sure as fuck hoped so. Fred needed medical care now.

"Send an ambulance to the ACE Hardware in Ashville. The owner's son is in bad shape. I think his dad beat the shit out of him."

"Jesus, not Fred Jr. His daddy's always been mean, but—hang on, okay, what can you tell me?"

Troy guessed that meant the EMS services were in Ashville since the operator knew who he was talking about. "I don't have much to tell you. I was going to the restrooms. I came out, heard a pitiful groan—" He didn't think telling the operator that he'd been snooping around was wise at all. "It sounded like someone was really hurting, so I came through the double doors and found him. I can't get a response from him now, though." Troy held the phone away and let the light from it reflect onto Fred. The kid was covered in bruises and blood. "Hurry, he's looking bad. I don't know—"

"What the fuck are you doing here?"

The shout almost had Troy dropping his phone, but he managed to keep his grip as Fred Sr thundered towards him. "Better send two ambulances," he said as the light came on and he saw Fred Sr's bloody, bandaged knuckles. Troy saw red as the older man lunged at him, swinging hard. He dropped his phone and let out a roar that matched his attacker's, ready to defend himself and Fred Jr from the raving lunatic.

Chapter Ten

Will ran down the sidewalk along with what had to be half the town. Sirens blared in the distance, but they didn't sound far away. He didn't question how everyone seemed to know bad shit was going down at the hardware store. It was a small town—news was carried in the air in some weird-ass small-town ritual. Whatever, however, he knew from the others around him that Fred Jr had been hurt and one of the 'new queers' in town was whaling on Fred Sr. Will's heart slammed against his ribs. He got more than one nasty comment as he shoved people out of the way, but damn it, they needed to fucking *move* out of his way!

Will's smaller stature came in handy. He slipped between people as the ambulance pulled up in front of the hardware store. Moving fast, not wanting to get blocked out, Will ran inside and began shoving through the spectators there. A dozen or so people were crammed at a doorway in the back. Will made a beeline for it, grunts and curses crackling in the store.

"Let me by," he snarled at a couple of men standing shoulder to shoulder.

"Fag," one of them snarled back. Will ducked a punch and slammed his fist into the man at kidney level. The man yelled and hit the floor. Will gave the other guy a glare, but the man raised his hands up as if to ward off an attack.

"I ain't like him." The man gestured with his chin to the downed form on the floor.

"Good," Will huffed as he went into the room. He'd have said more, but he saw Troy, straddling a giant of a man who was cussing and bucking. Troy sat on his chest and had his knees pinning the guy's arms. Fred Sr, Will guessed, and Troy had his wrists, too. There was blood running down from a gash at the corner of Troy's left eye, but the bastard on the floor didn't have a mark on his ugly face. And that man kept jerking, twisting, kicking—Troy was having a hell of a time holding on to him.

Will didn't call out. He knew better than to distract Troy, doing so could cost Troy his life. The man he held down was in a rage, froth and spittle flying from his foul mouth. Troy grimaced and grunted and held on. Will looked past him when he heard a pain-filled whimper. His stomach twisted into hot shaky knots as he saw a kid beaten black and blue, blood smeared from too many places to tell where the original wounds were. Two women and a man were with him, trying to help the poor guy.

Will turned his attention back to Troy as shouts from the EMS crew rang out, ordering people to clear the way. It was the distraction Will had feared, and Troy looked up at the additional noise.

Everything moved in a blur, Troy's eyes widening, the man beneath him freeing himself enough to throw a mean punch. Will shouted, and he wasn't the only one, but he didn't know if the others were cheering or screaming in protest as he dove forward. Troy's breath just burst out of him, like he'd been hit with a demolition ball. He came up several inches off the other guy's body, then he was toppling to the side.

Will found himself amidst a crowd all over again. Confusion warred with fear and fury as he tried to get to Troy. That man would kill him, Will could see it in the hateful fucker's eyes. Will battled the bodies and his own panic, managing to get to Troy just as two other men did. He yelled in a rage, thinking they were going after his man. No fucking way was he letting them hurt Troy!

"Get out of my freakin' way!" Will snarled at the men grabbing Troy. He was vaguely aware of other people grappling with the man who'd hit Troy, but that just wasn't his point of concern right then. He pushed at a smelly guy in front of him, pressing him sideways. Will was grabbed and yanked backwards, his feet actually leaving the floor. "What the fuck—"

"They ain't hurtin' him." Minty tobacco breath wafted over his cheek and assaulted his nose. Will snorted, doubt and the need to get that stank out of his sinus passages both at play. "I'm serious, little man. They tryin' to help him and t'others are holdin' Fred down to keep him from attackin' again. Ain't no one wantin' to see yer, uh, yer..."

"Partner," Will snapped. "He's my partner, my husband, my lover—"

"Got it, okay?" said his—Will didn't even know what the guy was. A good Samaritan trying to keep him out of harm's way?

Whatever. He smells like hogs and I hate the way chewing tobacco smells. "Let me go, you ass."

"Aw now, I can't do that, and it ain't nice ta call names."

Will craned his head around and glared. The guy holding onto him was about the size of Troy, and young-ish. He had a scroungy-looking blond beard and bright blue eyes. He had on a ratty straw hat and overalls, a cardinal sin as far as Will was concerned. "If you don't let me go, I will hurt you."

The blond guy's eyebrows shot up, but he didn't let go. "Ya promise not to try to kill Fred? The cops'll take care of him. I think that's why yer man there didn't beat the shit outta him."

"Really. The cops." Will couldn't hide his scorn. "I haven't been impressed at all by Sheriff Bowman yet."

"Aw, it ain't the sheriff that'll be showin'. It'll be Ashville's finest. We do have a police force here, even if it is just three men to it."

Will supposed they were out of the city limits at the Mossy Glenn, which was why they got the stupid fucking sheriff instead of Ashville's finest. He wasn't going to worry about it now. "Let me go, please. I need to check on Troy. He was hit hard."

"Yep, he sure was. Fred hits like he wants to kill a man." The blond scowled, anger contorting his features. "Someone shoulda done somethin' about him a long time ago." He released Will and also got the men seeing to Troy to scoot over. "Let him down there. That feller belongs to him."

Apparently some of the townsfolk were decent people who didn't care who he loved. Some weren't. It was the same as pretty much anywhere Will had ever lived, and he could handle it. What he couldn't handle was for Troy to be hurting.

Will wedged himself in front of one of the men and put his hand on Troy's chest. Troy opened his right eye, his left swollen almost shut, and looked right at him. Will's heart pinched with pain at seeing Troy bruised and bleeding, but damn it, he was so relieved that Troy was alive. Will couldn't hold back the tears, couldn't keep in the sob as he leant down. Troy reached for him, getting one shaking arm around Will's neck and tugging him down.

"I'm all right," Troy wheezed, not sounding all right at all to Will.

"You're hurt," Will argued, letting himself be brought down until his head rested on Troy's chest, his ear right over his heart. He tipped his face up so he could partially see Troy's face. Will put his arms around Troy as best as he could in such a position. He could only get his fingers under Troy's shoulders, but he did his best to hold on to him.

"Just bruised." Troy petted his back in a long stroke. "I didn't hit that fucker. Didn't want to go to jail."

"Yep, we can vouch for that."

Will ignored whoever was intruding on his private—fuck the crowd—conversation with Troy. "But you're bleeding, too, by your eye. And he hit you so hard I thought he popped your lung or something."

Troy's chest shook and he made a godawful sound that took Will a second or two to recognise as laughter. "Fuckin' thought he popped both of them." He coughed and groaned. "Damn, that hurts."

"Troy..." Will began, pushing himself up on his hands so he could better see Troy's face. "You might have broken ribs. They can puncture—"

"No." Troy closed his eyes for a moment and Will thought he had passed out until he looked at Will again. "Not broken. Been there, done that, and this isn't nearly as agonising. In fact, I can get up if you'll help."

Will opened his mouth to argue, only to be beaten to it by a familiar, annoying voice.

"Now, now, ya need ta stay right there and git looked over."

"Fuck off, blondie," Will growled, glaring to his left at the fashion disaster.

"It's Barney," the blond drawled. "Like the dinosaur, 'cept he's punier than me."

"Smarter, too, I'd bet." Will was still angry at being held back by the jerk. "Troy, you need to let the EMS people check you over. They're seeing to Fred Jr right now, but you'll be next."

"There's another crew comin' in right now." Barney grinned when Will glared. "Jus' tryin' to help."

Will was too bitchy for words, his emotions rampaging from the adrenaline. "You can help by butting out!"

He might have felt bad if Barney hadn't looked pleased as a bee buried in pollen. Was the guy just trying to piss him off? If so, he was succeeding.

"Clear out, folks. Let us do our jobs. Barney, get out of the way."

Will smirked at Barney. "Shoo."

"You too, sir."

Barney smirked back.

Will was going to find the big oaf and trip him just to watch him fall.

Will stroked Troy's cheek. "I need to let them check you over, okay? I'll be right here." He scooted back and watched as Troy was examined, his gaze never leaving Troy's except when Troy had to look at the medics or someone got between them.

"He really will be okay."

Will sighed grudgingly as Barney sat down beside him. "Why are you bugging me?" He guessed the oaf shrugged before answering since one of his shoulders jostled Will.

"Got nuthin' else to do, an' ya needed distractin' earlier 'fore ya got yer fella killed. Found out pokin' at ya was fun then. Now I'm gonna wanna do it every time I see ya."

Will narrowed his eyes, but didn't turn to Barney. "Are you always such an ass?"

"Guess so."

As suddenly as it'd hit him, Will's anger drained away, probably with the adrenaline, he figured. He felt exhausted and weak and fuzzy-headed, but he kept his spine straight. He wasn't going to let Barney see any weakness – but he also owed the guy an apology.

"I'm not usually so mean," Will admitted. "Sorry for that."

Another shrug, this one almost knocking Will sideways. He slapped a hand to the floor to keep from toppling over. "Sorry 'bout that. Yer little."

Will was fairly certain Barney was trying to irritate him. Whether it was to distract Will from worrying over Troy or not, he couldn't say. He could, however, put an end to the 'little' shit. "Barney, I'm not little where it counts. I've got a dick that'd make yours weep with envy."

When Barney didn't have a comeback for that, Will was tempted to check his expression, but the female medic turned to him then and waved him over. Will finally looked at someone other than Troy. "He's going to be okay, right?"

"We'd like him to get his ribs x-rayed, but he's refusing."

Will glared at Troy, who shook his head. "Not happening. I know my body, and I know the difference between broken ribs and just being walloped. There's nothing broke in there."

Will had no choice but to trust that Troy was right. He wouldn't challenge Troy's claims, at least not in front of strangers.

"He could be right, but we're always cautious," the medic said. "I bandaged his eye where Fred's knuckle tore the skin, and he's going to be black and blue by this evening. He needs to take it easy for a few days, and rest those ribs even if it's just a bruise." She took some papers from her partner and handed them to Will. "Here's some aftercare directions about concussions, in case he has one, and how to handle bruised ribs. Just because we didn't see any obvious signs of a concussion doesn't mean there isn't one, and he's declined x-rays for that as well. We don't know near enough about head injuries, so watch him closely, and call 911 if there's any sign of him losing consciousness or having trouble breathing."

"Yes, ma'am." Will folded the papers and tucked them in his back pocket.

"Have him seen by his regular physician tomorrow just to be safe. If he doesn't have one yet, there's two doctors here in Ashville, Doctor Viglio and Doctor Shepherd. Both are good at their jobs."

"Thank you. Thank you so much." Will helped Troy sit up when she left. He stood and held out his hand to Troy. Another hand appeared in his peripheral vision. Will and Troy both turned to see who it was and Will rolled his eyes at Barney. "Troy, Barney. I'll explain to you how we met later."

Troy let them help him up, which told Will just how shitty Troy must be feeling. "Maybe we should get you to one of those doctors for some pain medicine—"

Troy cut him off with a slash of his hand. "Whisky'll do it."

"Best painkiller ever," Barney chimed in.

Will bit back the impulse to ask Barney why he was still there. Will knew he was still cranky from being scared, and he didn't want to keep being a bitch about everything.

Besides, he imagined this was the most excitement Barney had seen in Ashville.

"Cops are here," someone called out from somewhere in the store. Will hooked an arm around Troy's waist.

"Come on, you're wobbly. How about you sit down on one of these boxes?"

Will noticed then that Fred Jr was gone, and he hoped it was only in the temporary sense.

"Ambulance took off with him a while ago," Barney told them, looking out of the double doors as he took off that battered hat and rolled the brim in his hands. "Freddie didn't look so good. His daddy really went too far this time."

"This time?" Will spat out. "Why the hell didn't anyone put a stop to the abuse if people knew about it?"

Troy looked at him and Will closed his eyes, drooping a little as he did so. He knew good and well why no one put a stop to it—because that was just how most people were. They didn't want to get involved, and for the victim—goddamn, he hated that word—pride and shame kept them silent. After a while, you just figured it was what you deserved for being stupid enough to put up with the beatings in the first place. At least, that was Will's experience.

"Never mind." Will opened his eyes and refused to look at Barney. They helped Troy to a seat on boxes across the room from the ones Fred Jr had been on. "Did you hear them say if Fred—er, Freddie—was going to be okay?"

Barney kicked at the floor with one very scuffed boot and twisted that hat so much Will figured it'd be shredded. "Naw, I dunno. Ain't like they'd tell me anythin' at the hospital, either."

That got Will's attention on the blond. He checked and sure enough Barney's cheeks were a vibrant shade of red. Will glanced at Troy, who arched his brows then whimpered and pressed a hand to his forehead.

"Don't do that, honey," Will told him, bending over and kissing his brow.

"Where's the man Kenny was talking about, the—" Will turned, still bent, and spotted two men entering the room. From their uniforms and badges, it was a sure bet they were the local cops. Will wondered what the older one had been about to say before cutting himself off so suddenly.

"There's the guy."

Well, if it'd been anything bad, Will couldn't tell. The older cop didn't sound disgusted or look all snooty and judge-y.

"I'm Officer Sweeny, and this is my partner, Officer McCain."

The younger office, McCain, looked as stoic as a human could possibly be. It was unnerving, and Will wondered if they'd have trouble with the man, or if he was just that emotionless with everyone. Officer Sweeny was friendly and professional as he asked Troy questions. Barney stayed with them, which was either endearing or weird, Will couldn't decide which. Officer McCain did his Oscar-worthy performance of a block of marble. Will wasn't even sure he was breathing.

"Thank you." Officer Sweeny held out his hand and shook Troy's first, then Will's. "Sorry this happened. Ashville usually isn't like this. We're a peaceful little town."

"Maybe too peaceful," Will muttered. Sweeny looked at him and the living statue, Officer McCain, blinked. Will decided to explain himself briefly. "Look, I grew up being abused. I have scars from it. It kept on until—" Oh, he couldn't bring in both his men. A ménage even involving straight folks wouldn't go over with most of society. "Until Troy and our friend Carlos helped me to understand I didn't have to put up with it. I didn't *deserve* it. If they hadn't stepped in, I might have ended up dead eventually, either from my own father, or myself"—Will patted Troy's leg when Troy inhaled sharply—"because I wouldn't have given a damn about living." He looked from Sweeny to McCain, and thought he saw something stirring in the depths of the man's icy blue eyes. "My question is, if everyone here knew what was happening to Fred Jr, then why didn't anyone try to stop it? Because when it was me, I don't think anyone outside of immediate family was aware of what was going on. I was sheltered, and yeah, I made sure to cover the bruises and burns up. I helped my father get away with it, because that's how I was raised. But when someone cared enough to intervene..." Will didn't say anything more. Either the cops would get it or they wouldn't.

Sweeny didn't look quite so friendly now. "Well, things work different in small towns." He turned and left. McCain watched him for a half a second more then did the same.

"Fred, his brother's got the biggest ranch in the state," Barney added. "Means they got money. Intimidates people, ya know." Barney smiled, making his plump cheeks pop. "Lines pockets, too. I'll be surprised if ol' Fred serves much time at all."

Will tilted his head and tapped his chin with one finger. "Hm. You know what, Barney? We have a good friend who retired from the FBI. It's about time we called and saw how Glenn and James are doing, right Troy?"

Barney's eyes were so huge Will didn't get why they hadn't just popped right on out of his head. "Yer sure gonna keep this town innerestin', ain't ya?" Barney asked almost reverently. "I thought ya was lyin' about havin' a big willy, but now I think ya meant it. Gotta have some balls the size of Texas to go with it."

"Why were y'all discussing your huge dick?" Troy asked. "Did he make a joke about your height or something?"

Will cut his eyes at Barney. "He kept calling me little."

Troy snorted then groaned and cupped his face in his hands. "Aw, fuck. Fuck, that hurt."

"I'd be happy ta help ya to yer truck," Barney offered.

Will wasn't too proud to accept. Together they got Troy to his feet, and Will realised there had been people lingering by the door eavesdropping when they scattered like roaches spotlighted at midnight in a dumpster. One of them didn't scatter, though, and Will faced him as they walked out. "Yes?" It came out slightly snarky, but he was glad he hadn't been outright obnoxious when the guy offered him a smile.

"I was mixing the paint for your partner when all hell broke loose."

Will winced then, noticing the red work vest the man had on. "Sorry. Didn't mean to snap."

He waved Will off. "Aw, naw, it's understandable. I just wanted you to know that I'll bring the paint out myself here shortly. I think we're closing up for the day, considering."

"That'd be real nice of you, appreciate it." Will was in a hurry to get Troy home since Troy wasn't a lightweight and he was leaning heavily on Will. Later he'd be more polite. "Thanks again."

Barney didn't yammer at the guy like Will feared he might, and they had Troy outside in no time at all. There were more people out on the sidewalks than Will had seen before, but he supposed that was the way it was everywhere.

"Hey, why don't ya let me hold yer fella up and you can go get yer truck?" Barney asked, almost glowing with pride over his idea. "Be easier on Troy."

"It would," Troy agreed, "but I'm not so hurt I can't fucking walk."

"Now that'd be somethin' to see, fuckin' and walkin'."

Will just about swallowed his tongue when Barney made that comment. Troy let out a bark of laughter that caused him to groan again, and Barney's face was flaming red. Will guessed he hadn't meant to blurt that out. He wondered if Barney was gay, but it wasn't any of his business so he told himself to stop wondering. Yeah, Barney had seemed really…attached, to Freddie, as he called him. That could just be because they had been buddies in school. Lord knew Barney looked like the sports type, and so did Freddie. They'd probably been on all sorts of teams together.

The walk to the truck took only a few minutes longer than it would have if Troy hadn't been hurt, but part of that was because of the people who stopped and thanked him. Six times, Troy was told how grateful someone was because he put an end to 'poor Freddie's' abuse. Will ground his teeth every time. He was glad people appreciated Troy's actions, but damn it, they should have stepped in before it got to that point.

Will's phone buzzed in his back pocket. He yelped from the surprise of it, having forgotten all about the damned thing. When his stopped, Troy's front pocket chimed.

Troy grunted as they eased him into the truck. "Bet that's Carlos."

"I'll call him, don't worry about getting your phone out of your pocket. You're lucky that snap didn't come undone while you were playing wrestle the fuckwit on the floor."

"Don't make me laugh, Will. Hurts." Troy winced and Will hoped his contrition showed when he kissed Troy's temple.

"Sorry. I'll stop being my usual amazing, entertaining self. It'll be hard, though."

"Uh."

Will and Troy almost smacked their heads together as they looked at Barney. Will had kind of pretty much forgotten about him.

"Thanks for the help, Barney." Will started to buckle Troy in but Troy caught his hand. Will glared at Troy for a second before looking at Barney and asking, "There's air bags in this thing, and deer trying to get us to hit them and fuck up our trucks, right, Barney?"

Barney giggled and slapped a hand over his mouth. "Mmhm."

Will was thrown off by a guy that size giggling, but he tried not to show it. "If I can't buckle you in, you need to be in the back seat. Might be better anyway, so you can lie down."

Troy moaned and started getting out of the truck. "The lying down part sounds like a plan, but the moving part kinda sucks."

Once Troy was lying down, Will shut the door and Barney was right *there,* in the way. Will looked up at the jolly blond giant. "Thanks again."

"Yer welcome." Barney had his hat in his hands and was twisting it all around again. "I was wonderin', maybe I could come help ya paint later? I ain't got nowhere to be, and it just ain't right that yer place keeps getting' messed with. Someone ought to help ya out."

Will studied Barney, wondering at his motivation for helping. In the end, it didn't matter. They could use the help, but Barney needed to know something first. "You do know that we've hired family—we've got the LGB part of the rainbow, but we're more than happy to add on. Just haven't got the funds to hire more people yet, but when we do, they'll be people who need a safe place to work and be themselves."

Barney gulped, but he didn't look away or walk off. That counted for something in Will's book.

"You could ride out with the guy from the hardware store, help him bring all the paint out, if you want." Will teetered on the verge of offering Barney a ride, but maybe the guy had his own vehicle, and Will really needed some alone time with his men. His phone kept buzzing and he knew Carlos was going to rightfully let him have an earful for not calling already. "I've got to go, sorry. Carlos is going to flip out already. Look." Will grabbed a paper and pen from the glove box and jotted down his number. He hadn't seen Barney pull out a cell phone, and he wasn't going to hang around wasting any more time. "Here's my number. Do you have a vehicle?"

Barney shook his head and his face flamed again.

Will understood a man's pride. He had plenty himself, so he just went on talking. "Okay, no big. If you can't or don't want to ride with the guy from the store, just give me a call after an hour or so. I need to get Troy home, and I need to spend some time with him, but I can send someone to pick you up."

Barney's lips parted and Will thought he was going to finally speak again, but instead he just nodded and stepped back.

Will felt like he should be helping Barney, somehow, but he had two men who needed him. Carlos was going to be angry, but he wouldn't be a dick. That wasn't Carlos' way. Still, he'd need some lovin', and so would Troy, and God knew Will needed the reassurance that both his men were alive and well and loving him. He got in the truck and started it, then headed for home.

Chapter Eleven

Every time Carlos looked at Troy, he thought about how they could have lost him. Troy's eye was swollen shut, and he had a colourful patch of bruises on his face and ribs. Carlos knew he'd recover, but his mind kept dancing to what-ifs. He knew the foolishness of that, yet he couldn't make himself stop.

Him and Will had spent most of the day inside with Troy despite Troy's claims he should be working. It wasn't happening, and Carlos had made sure Troy understood that. The ranch hands had been joined by a handful of townsfolk, which had touched Carlos and his partners.

Will had been disappointed that the guy who'd helped him get Troy to the truck hadn't shown up, but Carlos was just glad for the show of acceptance they got from the volunteers. The barns had been painted in no time flat, and Carlos had stepped outside to offer his thanks and coffee, along with returning the favour should any of the kind people need it. It had truly been an amazing experience, even if Carlos hadn't been out amongst everyone doing it. He had tried, but Rocky and Salt had run him back inside. Granted, he'd wanted to be with Troy, or else no one would have chased him off.

As the sun set, Carlos settled deeper into the comfy chair they'd bought for their bedroom. Will was cuddling with Troy, both of them drooling and just looking adorable. Carlos wouldn't let anyone hurt them again. He'd failed Troy today, and it didn't matter if that was logical or not. Carlos was older, he was what a lot of people would call a Dom. He didn't care what the title was. When it came down to it, he was the protective man who loved Will and Troy more than should have been possible. Carlos would do anything for them.

And if Fred Sr ended up a free man, that was going to be a problem.

He watched them sleep for another half hour, then Carlos quietly stood and left the bedroom. In the kitchen, Drake was puttering around, making something for supper. He'd been subdued all day, quiet, which wasn't like him. Whatever was bothering Drake, it was his own business unless he chose to share it. Carlos wouldn't push, unless Drake started slacking on the job.

"What ya got going?" Carlos asked him, taking in the diced tomatoes and lettuce on the table. Drake had worked hard outside all day, so Carlos had told him he could skip fixing supper tonight, but Drake had insisted. Carlos wasn't dumb enough to argue.

"Just tacos, if that's okay." Drake nodded towards part of the counter covered in flour. "I'm making homemade tortillas. Haven't done it in ages, but I think they'll turn out decent."

Carlos' mouth watered at the promise of tacos. He hadn't had any since they'd left Texas, and he'd got to where he'd craved them when he'd lived there. "I've been in taco withdrawal. What kind are you making?"

Drake lifted the lid off a skillet. "Carne guisada, some cheater fajitas, and chorizo and egg."

Carlos came over to the stove and stood beside Drake, but not so close as to be inappropriate. There were only two men he wanted to touch. "How the hell do you make cheater fajitas?"

"By using the already cooked frozen ones you can buy at the grocery store." Drake pointed the spatula towards a bag in the trash can. "They aren't as good as home-cooked, but I added plenty of seasoning and they aren't half bad, either. Slather on guacamole and salsa and you're good to go."

"We have salsa?"

Drake smiled a little, looking more like the guy Carlos knew him to be. "Made some up earlier. That new blender sure does run quiet."

"Must do, I didn't hear it." Carlos went to the blender and took the lid off. He sniffed. His nose burned and his eyes watered. He caught the aroma of jalapenos and spices. "This smells great." His mouth wasn't the only thing watering, his eyes were doing it, too.

"It's going to be really spicy." Drake handed him a paper towel. "I made a wussier version for anyone not up to real hot sauce."

The reappearance of Drake's personality cheered Carlos up considerably, and they chatted for a while as Drake cooked. Carlos kept his eyes mostly on the doorway in case either of his men woke up, but it didn't happen.

"Supper'll be ready in ten," Drake said as he began setting the table.

"I gotta make a call, then I'll get Will, and Troy if he's up to moving. If he ain't, I'll take him supper." Then something dawned on him. "Did you make the tortillas 'cause they're soft and easier to chew than the crunchy kind?"

Drake shrugged one shoulder. "Partially, and partially I just wanted to make them."

"Thanks for thinking of Troy." Carlos was glad Drake had done so. "I'm going to step out on the porch to talk."

"Gotcha. Privacy." Drake saluted him with the spatula.

Carlos went outside. It was chilly, bordering on outright cold, but still bearable without a jacket. The porch light was on and he turned it off, wanting to see the pitch black sky and the millions of stars freckling it. Texas had some beautiful night skies, but Montana had it beat, at least in Carlos' opinion. He stepped off the porch and looked up, pivoting slowly. There was nothing like all that beauty, that wide-open space, so endless and dark and bright above you, to make you humble. He wasn't even a shining speck like the smallest star.

Carlos rubbed the back of his neck as it twinged then he

brought his thoughts and his gaze back down to Earth. Will had mentioned calling Glenn earlier, and Carlos thought it was a good idea. He wasn't real close to the guy, but he did know him and pretty much all of their friends in Texas were linked somehow or another.

Glenn answered promptly and said he wasn't busy after Carlos asked him, so Carlos explained what had gone down in Ashville earlier.

"Will said the father was supposed to be related to the richest rancher in the state."

"Ugh. Rich men tend to give me the willies after what we've been through."

Carlos got that, he sure enough did. Glenn's husband James had been a lawyer for a rich, crooked man who'd used his money and power to destroy everyone he could. James had been one of his victims, and Carlos had heard snippets about torture and sexual abuse, but he didn't know more than that. Didn't want to, either. There wasn't no purpose in anyone spilling James' secrets to him. Glenn had been with the FBI at the time. He'd been the man who'd found James.

"Will did some research online and said the guy's gearing up for a political career. Gonna run for senator. I wouldn't think he'd want bad press, and surely it'd be worse if it came out he was letting his brother get away with beating on his kid."

"Maybe," Glenn agreed. "Let me make a few calls, see what I can find out. I still have friends in the Bureau, and if a little pressure from them can ensure fair jail time for this Fred, then I'll do my best to get it done. I can't stand a bully."

"Me either." Carlos finished up the call then went in. He stopped by the kitchen. "I'll get 'em up if I can," he told Drake, who hummed in approval.

In the bedroom, the soft light from the bedside lamp shone on Troy and Will. Carlos woke Troy first with a soft kiss on those parted lips. Troy opened one eye, the other not up to the task. "Uhn?"

"Supper, if you want it. Drake made soft tacos."

"Supper?" Will slurred, raising his head up. "I'm starving. Ugh. Slobber." He rubbed his face on Troy's chest.

Carlos ruffled Will's hair, feeling near to bursting with love for his men. "I can bring your supper in here, if you want. Might be best."

Will sat up and scooted off the bed. Troy reached for him and Carlos offered his hands, holding steady as Troy pulled himself upright. Pain splashed across Troy's face, and he was panting by the time he got his feet on the floor. He held one arm around his middle but waved off Carlos' suggestion of lying back down.

"I can't stand being laid up sick, or hurt. Freaks me out, and I won't be near as stiff if I move a little."

Carlos had got his share of bruises and breaks, too, and understood what Troy meant. He still offered his arm to Troy, and Troy took it. Will got on Troy's other side and even though they had to turn sideways to get through the doorways, they didn't let go of each other, each of them needing the comfort of the others.

Drake wasn't in the kitchen, but like some psychic chef, he'd put the bench seat on the front side of the table, along with their plates. A thick cushion made the bench just as nice a seat as the chairs, that and the high back to it.

"Guess Drake's not eating with us," Will said. "Damn, I feel awful. I forgot all about him being upset. Jeez. Did he seem okay to you?"

Carlos shook his head. "Seemed subdued for the most part, but after a while he perked up." He helped Troy get situated on the end of the bench. Will took the middle seat and Carlos the other end. "He might just need some time to himself to deal with whatever upset him this morning."

Will made a wordless sound then exclaimed at the Mexican food feast Drake had fixed them. "Oh my God, is that chorizo? I didn't even know we had chorizo in Montana! Yum! Troy, what kind of tacos do you want, two of each?"

"Yeah, except maybe half that," Troy replied. "Smother them in hot sauce too."

Troy liked medium heat, so Carlos pointed to the two bowls of it, one in a red ceramic dish and one in a clear bowl. "I'm thinking a mix of the two for him. One of those is hotter than Hell itself. Might want to sniff first, then hand me the one that'll sear my stomach lining."

Will slanted him a knowing look. "You're sleeping on top of the blankets tonight."

Carlos laughed—how could he not? The meal was good, the hot sauce perfect, and the company even more so. Despite Troy's battered appearance and sore ribs, he started making suggestions about how the evening should end. Since all of them involved him watching for the most part, Carlos saw no reason to shoot down the man's ideas. Troy did like to watch, and Will loved being the centre of attention. Carlos enjoyed keeping them both happier than pigs in mud.

Carlos wanted to take care of Will and Troy after their experience in Ashville. "You two just sit there and relax, I'll clean up the kitchen."

"Ooo, I likey," Will purred. "If you could just do it naked, everything would be perfect."

"Perfect's boring," Carlos shot back, winking at Will. "Use your imagination, and think of what I could do with this spatula."

Carlos got started clearing plates, then he put the food up. Will batted his lashes and groped Troy off and on. Troy reciprocated, and Carlos enjoyed seeing the two of them playing around.

Drake's door opened and he stepped out, eyes red-rimmed and hair all willy-nilly. He wore sweats that accentuated his thick legs and package, and a T-shirt torn at the neck. Carlos wasn't the only one looking at their cook. The man looked like he felt like shit.

"I thought you all would be, uh, done." Then Drake's

eyes went wide and he darted over to Carlos. "What are you doing? Don't! I was gonna clean the kitchen up, I promise—"

"Calm down," Carlos told him in his firmest voice. Drake froze and dropped his gaze. "I don't know what's got you in a lather, but if I'd thought you were shirking your duties, I'd have said so. Ain't no reason I can't give you a break, and frankly, you look like you've been put through the wringer and lit on fire. You want to talk about what's got your eyes all puffy?"

Carlos hadn't known he was going to make the offer. Hadn't he just been thinking it wasn't his business unless Drake brought it to him? But Drake had seemed on the verge of flipping his lid over Carlos doing a few dishes, and that was just bizarre in Carlos' opinion.

"I don't want to talk about it."

Well, that was what Carlos had figured. Still, he had to offer. "If you change your mind, you can talk to all of us or any one of us. We don't keep secrets from each other, but if you confide in, say, Will, we won't be throwing your secret in your face."

Drake looked up at him, reluctance evident in the slow way he did it. "Tomorrow, okay? I just… I need to think, and I could tell when I walked in here that you all had plans."

Carlos doubted that. Drake had looked caught off guard to find them in the kitchen still, and he'd about had a panic attack. Calling him on it wasn't going to happen though. "Okay, but only if you want. It ain't a job requirement." He stopped short of telling Drake he had friends here, because they hadn't yet got to that place where friendship and employment tangled up until it didn't matter much. Drake shuffled back into his room and closed the door. Carlos resumed washing the dishes.

When he finished and they were back in the bedroom, he made sure Troy was propped up comfortably after stripping him down. "Look at this pretty dick," he said to

Will, though he looked at Troy. Despite his injuries, Troy's cock was already starting to firm up. The thick, hot length of it always felt so good inside Carlos. If he thought he could ride Troy without making him hurt, he'd jump right on, but he wasn't risking it, not tonight.

"I love the way he uses it, too," Will said from where he waited at the foot of the bed. "He can get it so deep inside me I can feel it at the other end."

"Exaggerate much?" Troy asked around a quiet laugh. "I'm not as hung as Carlos."

Will crawled up onto the bed, kept right on until he was between Troy's legs. Troy's cock twitched and filled in Carlos' grip. Will put his mouth to good use, sucking the fat tip right in.

"Ungh." Troy arched his neck and covered his eyes with one hand. "Feels good."

"I bet it does." Carlos let Will suck the tip for a while, until Troy started to squirm. "Can't have you hurting yourself," he told Troy as he nudged Will's chin.

Will left off with a lewd pop. His chin was shiny with spit and his lips swollen and red. Carlos didn't think he was going to be able to keep rein on his usual control tonight. He grabbed Will under one arm and lifted him right up off the bed.

"Fuck him hard," Troy rasped, fondling his cock, working that tip and right under the cap. "Make him scream for it."

Someone was feeling the need for rough again. Of course, Will loved it, loved being pounded into. Troy generally liked slow and easy when it was him being fucked, but there was the occasional exception, like the night Carlos had tied him up. Judging by Troy's demands, he was wanting more of the same again.

Will was already whimpering for it. His cock was dripping pre-cum all over the place and Carlos was going to make use of it.

"Better milk this out, 'cause it's all I'm using." He massaged Will's dick once he had him bent over the side of the bed. Will moaned for him, his body shaking as Carlos gathered up the pre-cum. "You hold on, and I'll fuck you through two rounds."

Will lowered himself until his shoulders were on the bed and his pert ass up in the air. His ass cheeks spread and Carlos saw that tight little pucker. He looked at Troy and grinned, then he delved right in, licking a stripe down Will's crack.

"Yes! Fuck! Eat me, please," Will begged.

Carlos pulled one cheek back and left off teasing Will's dick. He'd get him wet this way instead. He smacked Will's ass hard enough to leave a mark. Troy made a sound almost like the one that slipped past Will's lips, a needy, breathy exhalation full of need.

Carlos slapped Will's ass again, pulling back from eating him out long enough to see the impact of hand to flesh. A third slap brought Will up on his toes, a shout leaving him. His ass clenched and the scent of cum reached Carlos.

"Uh uh. You weren't supposed to come yet." Another swat, harder than the last. Will's ass was dark red, even purple in a few spots.

"You—you know I can't stop it," Will panted. "I can't, I can't—"

Carlos did know that. He wasn't mad—this was all part of the way they played together. "Still, you were supposed to wait. Now I'm gonna have to think about fucking you as long as I wanted to. I might just fuck your face first, then plough this sweet ass." Another spank, not as hard, because Will was already going to be feeling the swats tomorrow, and likely the day after, too. The thought of burying his dick in Will's throat was enough to have Carlos' control wavering. He pushed Will's cheeks apart until his hole gaped then he licked into it, teasing them both.

Will keened and cursed, begged and bucked for him. Carlos finally flipped him over then dragged him around until his head hung off the bed. His feet were close to Troy's ribs, but not the injured side, so Carlos wasn't too worried about Will kicking, especially not when Troy started caressing his legs.

"Open up for me," Carlos said as he rubbed his cockhead all over Will's face. Will moaned and started to bring his hands up. "Nuh uh. You can use those on your tits, make 'em pretty and rosy for us while I'm taking your mouth." He put on his sternest expression. "What do you do if it's too much and you need me to stop?"

"Tap the bed if my mouth's full, Red if it isn't."

There wasn't normally a need for safe words between them, but on occasion when there was something new or risky to be tried, Carlos made sure his men were aware and on board with him in regards to safety.

Confident that Will would be responsible, and that he himself would be cautious, Carlos lined his cock up and sank it into the moist heat of Will's mouth.

The sounds Will made were maddening as Carlos pushed past his lips again and again. Will's tongue never ceased to flick all along his length, urging him on. Carlos cupped Will's head, giving him some support, and he began pushing deeper, breaching his throat.

His balls slapped against Will's face, covering his nose for precious seconds before he pulled back. Carlos was careful, paying little heed to his own pleasure no matter how good Will sucked him.

Will had hinted and flat-out asked for more breathplay, and Carlos was giving it to him, although on Carlos' terms. He knew all too well that sometimes what you fantasised about turned out to be a nightmare in reality. He had been through that with cock-and-ball torture. He used to get off thinking about having it done, but he'd tried it in his younger days and had absolutely hated it.

Will's nipples were getting a harsher workout than Carlos normally gave them. Will was whimpering around his cock, and every time Carlos pushed in and let his balls rest over Will's nose, Will just about twisted his titty plumb off.

Troy wasn't quiet either. His breath was coming in

choppy waves as he rubbed the head of his cock faster and faster. His gaze was glued to Will's mouth, and Carlos' dick filling it.

"Jerk off," Carlos ordered as he pulled back. Will grabbed his cock and tugged with one hand while keeping the other on one red, pointy tip. "Show Troy how much you love this." Carlos pushed in again, a steady drive into Will's throat. Will swallowed around him and Carlos cursed, his climax boiling up and trying to burst forth.

Will's cock spewed again, and Carlos jerked back, letting his balls drag heavy over Will's face. Before Will's cock stopped shooting, Carlos had him pulled around and bent over the bed again. He needed to fuck Will and come *now*.

Carlos lined his cock up and thrust. Will's body sucked his cock right in, burying it in silky, rippling heat. Will keened and rocked back, but Carlos pressed down on his back at his shoulder and above his hip. He needed, and Will was giving it to him. Carlos held him down while Will mumbled a litany of "yeses" and "fuck me harders".

Carlos did, watching his cock split Will's ass open for several thrusts before looking at Troy, watching him splatter cum all over the place.

"Harder," Troy said after he stopped shaking and coming. "Damn, look at you two."

Carlos couldn't see much of anything then, because Will's ass clamped down so tight on him it stole his breath and possibly stopped his heart. He slammed in and froze, cum pouring out of his cock and into Will. Carlos jerked when Will's inner walls spasmed around his length, pulling another spurt of jizz from him. He was just going to collapse onto the floor once he could make himself pull his dick free of Will's warm body.

That plan was trashed once Carlos' mind cleared a bit. He helped Will onto the bed, covering him with his own body even though his cock slipped out. The bed was wet and cold in spots, but he was worn out, and Will was supple and warm against him. Carlos sighed contentedly and peeked at Troy, not surprised to find him out again.

They'd all be sticky messes in the morning, and likely have to peel the blankets and sheets off them, but that was all right. Carlos closed his eyes and let sleep steal him away with his men.

Chapter Twelve

Three days after nearly having his ribs cracked, Troy was feeling almost human again. His ribs would be tender for a while, but that was nothing compared to having them fractured or broken, both of which he'd experienced when he'd taken a turn on his dirt bike way too fast. He'd been seventeen and certain he could handle anything. He'd handled the pain of that injury by bawling and begging to be knocked out. The pain in his side was an annoyance rather than a searing agony, so Troy wasn't worried about it.

But damn, he wished he didn't look like someone had tried to tenderise the side of his face. His eye was still swollen, though not as bad as it had been. The bruising, however… Troy didn't even want to look at himself to shave. Tricky, considering he liked his head smooth to the touch. He'd never thought of himself as really vain, but seeing himself in the mirror turned his stomach.

If Will and Carlos hadn't been touching him and loving on him so much, Troy wasn't sure how he'd have handled being so ugly. At least with the dirt bike wreck, he'd had a helmet on his noggin.

Despite his rough appearance, or maybe because of it, Troy hadn't been in too many fights, and the ones he had been involved in had been over pretty quickly. Troy was fast, and he didn't like the idea of another man hitting him.

Except for Carlos, but that was totally not the same. Hitting them in anger was something Carlos would never do. What he did to them was consensual and so fucking hot it could have given the sun competition.

Troy walked out onto the porch to join Carlos for their morning cup of coffee.

"Getting some more cattle in today," Carlos said right before he nuzzled Troy's unbruised cheek. "Almost got as many as we need to get this place going right."

"That's good." Troy stood shoulder to shoulder with Carlos and sipped his coffee. The morning was chilly, and the heavy flannel shirt he had on wasn't quite heavy enough. He shivered and drank faster. Carlos moved closer and talked about the incoming cattle and the plans to put them in the east pasture first, along with numerous other ranch-related details. Troy hadn't learned as much as he'd hoped about ranching, but he would, eventually. He nodded and commented where he was supposed to, but his mind was jumpy this morning. He needed to get some exercise before his brain jumped right out of his skull.

"Will still talking with Drake?" Carlos asked him.

Troy frowned as he retraced his steps earlier. "Didn't see them in the kitchen. There's a stack of biscuits and pancakes on the stove, and I figured Will was off doing something, which is true enough. He's trying out help Drake out."

"Coulda mentioned that breakfast was done sooner." Carlos gave him a steely look that just served to make Troy's cock grow erect despite the cold. Carlos' lips twitched and he dropped his gaze. Troy felt it like a touch running over his body and settling on his groin. "You're about ready for me to ride, ain't you?"

At the thought of having Carlos riding his shaft, Troy almost came in his jeans. "You know it. Maybe at lunch, if we don't have a shitload of chores still?"

Carlos tipped his head and went inside. Troy took that for the 'yes' that it was and wondered how he was going to put up the security cameras Will had got in the mail yesterday with a boner. He'd be lucky if he didn't fall off the damn ladder and break his ribs.

The kitchen was empty when he and Carlos entered it. "Should we knock on Drake's door?" Troy asked.

Carlos shook his head. "Let 'em talk. Will knows we're out here. Neither one of us steps lightly on these wooden floors."

Troy brought the pancakes and biscuits to the table. Carlos brought a pot of gravy and a stack of sausages from the oven. A metal pitcher of orange juice was already on the table, along with four glasses. "I'm guessing Drake was planning to join us."

"Looks like," Carlos agreed as he loaded his plate. "I'm glad he's talking to Will, though. Hopefully he'll get whatever's been bothering him off his chest."

"Yeah." Troy ate a piece of bacon, chewing it slowly to enjoy that first flavour of man candy on his tongue.

"You think maybe you can call the hardware store and see if anyone there knows how that kid Fred is doing?"

"Yeah, I can do that." Another bite, then Troy continued talking. "Rocky told me no one knows for sure what set the old man off yet. She was talking to Rona in town, but that's all she's heard. Meant to tell you last night but Will jumped on you like a flea on a dog."

"Sucked me dry," Carlos said happily. "Then he blew your mind, too."

Troy grew warm from thinking about it. "He always does."

"Mmhm." Carlos looked past him, but his gaze was unfocused. "Ain't no telling what set that guy off, Troy. I know you told me Will had called right before that, but I don't think that had anything to do with it, do you?"

"Maybe. I heard Fred Sr hollering at his son. Maybe he thought—" Troy stopped short.

"Thought what?"

Troy rubbed his head, as if he could massage out the rest of that sentence. "I don't know what he thought. I can't comprehend doing what he did."

Carlos pushed his plate back a few inches and leaned against the table. "I can't either, but there's people in this world who are just plumb filled up with hate. Decent people won't ever understand that 'cause they aren't the same inside."

"I guess not." Troy stood, only wincing a little inside at the slow burn of pain along his side. "You know what time the cattle are coming?"

"Sometime in the afternoon. I'll call the delivery driver in another couple of hours and see if she's still on schedule." Carlos stood as well. "You ready to put those cameras up?"

"Yeah." Troy looked out over the land he could see. The Mossy Glenn itself was right at fifteen hundred acres. Carlos had said it used to be almost twice that before Antonia started selling off parts of it. Nick, Rory, and Annabelle, the owners of the place, had tried to buy back as much of it as they could, but money wasn't talking as fast as they'd like. The land was beautiful, mountains shadowing them on the North side of the property. Troy hadn't ridden out over all the land yet, but he hoped to once things were up and running at full steam.

"How many cattle will we have with the next load?"

"Six hundred, and that's pushing our maximum capacity until we get the soil in better shape and have more grass growing. We're gonna have to feed with hay more this time around and that'll hurt us. Grass is a helluva lot cheaper than hay." Carlos put his hand on Troy's shoulder. "I'll eventually have to go to the bank for Nick and them, do what most ranchers do and borrow money until we sell the calves. I don't see any other way with the three of them wanting to buy up the property to the west. If they'd leave it be, we'd be fine for the time being, but that's the way of ranching. Let's just hope things don't go to shit before the sell-off."

"I thought we were financially okay for now." Troy felt like his head couldn't hold all the new information he was learning, or trying to. "Sounds like ranching is more of a gamble than anything else."

"That's what makes it fun." Carlos grinned and started down the steps. "And we are all right money-wise, but if they want to shell out thousands for land because they're thinking more of their lost heritage than making what they do have a success, I can't stop 'em."

"Have you explained that to them?"

"Yep." Carlos stopped and tipped his head up, looking at the blue sky. "Maybe I should talk with Chance. He's less emotionally invested in this than the other three are."

Chance, Rory's husband of several years, was a level-headed man about the same age as Carlos. Rory was in his twenties and probably prone to making his decisions based on his emotions, Troy supposed. He didn't really know the guy very well.

An hour into setting up the cameras, Will came out. "Can you come talk with me for a few minutes?" Worry lines were etched around his eyes, and Troy wondered just how bad Drake's situation was.

"Yeah." He climbed down the ladder, joining Carlos, who'd been reading the directions to him again. Troy thumbed the fine lines and Will huffed.

"Damn it, I'm going to need Botox or something soon. Stress is *not* my friend."

"You look gorgeous and you know it," Troy told him.

Will tossed his hair back, the silky strands just brushing his shoulders. "I do not. Carlos is sexy as sin with his wrinkles. Those aren't even wrinkles—those are experience and intelligence put right out there for everyone to see. I'll just be a droopy old hag by the time I hit forty. But!" He flapped a hand. "This isn't about me."

"I was wondering if I should get offended there for a minute," Carlos muttered. "Experience and intelligence, my ass. This is just old age sitting on my face." He swiped a hand down his cheek. "But I look damned good carrying it."

Troy hoped he was as confident when he was Carlos' age.

"Not the porch," Will said, grabbing them each by one arm. "Drake's in the kitchen now, but I wouldn't want him walking out and hearing us."

"He knows you're going to tell us." Troy wasn't sure if he was arguing or clarifying. "How about we head to the second bunkhouse? Everyone there is out working pastures and fences. We should have privacy." He would *not* let his mind sink into the gutter, either. Will obviously had something serious to talk with them about.

"Sounds good."

The second bunkhouse was a small structure that slept six hands, two to each bedroom. It had a front porch—Troy figured that was a requirement on any ranch housing, no matter what state you lived in. The living room was just big enough to hold two couches, a chair, a coffee table and a flatscreen TV. He and Carlos sat down while Will took a quick peek to make sure they were alone, then he joined them, sitting on the coffee table and facing them where they sat on the couch.

Will sat cross-legged and folded his hands in his lap. "Well, it was like we talked about. Drake's ex was a cheating shithead, and he didn't bother being safe about it. Now he's HIV-positive, and Drake is scared out of his mind."

Just hearing it made Troy's insides go cold with fear. He couldn't imagine how Drake must feel. "He's getting tested, right?"

Will nodded. "He's afraid we'll fire him, especially if he is positive."

Troy looked at Carlos, who was frowning mightily. "We wouldn't do that, would we? We're not going to be those paranoid people who freak out despite knowing that HIV isn't contagious from someone safely handling our food?"

Carlos hesitated a second before shaking his head. "'Course not. I was trying to figure out what we could do about the insurance, health and on the ranch. I don't know what the laws are regarding our responsibilities, and who we do or don't have to let know if Drake is positive. I wouldn't kick a man when he's down."

Will bobbed his head. "That's what I told him, minus all the legal mumbo-jumbo. I offered to take him in to Bozeman for testing tomorrow, if that's okay with you both. He didn't want to try the at-home test, and he's taking this real seriously."

"Like he should," Carlos said. "It's not a joke."

"Nope, but there are too many people who think it's treatable like diabetes and such, and they don't stop to think that those things kill people too." Troy had heard it often enough in the club he'd been a bartender at. "It's not just gay men, either. I think most of the younger generations, mine included, have forgotten the eighties."

"I think you're right, but we don't know what anyone else is thinking." Carlos sighed and leant back on the couch, stretching his arms out. "Man, I meant what I said, I wouldn't fire Drake, but I sure hope he doesn't have it. That's a hard row to hoe for sure, and he seems like a nice guy."

"Yeah," Will agreed. He got up and insinuated himself between them, resting his head on Troy's shoulder. "You know, he told me that Rigo, his ex, is the only guy he'd been with other than some messing around when he was a kid."

Troy caressed Will's hair while reaching for Carlos with his other hand. The pain in his side was annoying, but didn't hamper him. "I am so fucking glad we found each other."

* * * *

After Troy installed the last camera and Will made sure he could see everything he wanted to on his laptop, Troy felt kind of proud of himself. He'd seen the security cameras being installed at the bar he'd worked in before meeting Will and Carlos, but he hadn't had anything to do with the installation.

Of course, he'd forgotten about the cameras when Will and Carlos had tempted him into the storage room. Fuck, but that'd been hot, Carlos all commanding and strong… Troy shivered, his groin warming as arousal stirred. They'd accidentally made a sex tape, and ever since, Troy had wondered about making one on purpose. He could just imagine watching Carlos fuck him on video while he fucked the stuffing out of Will—or Carlos. Carlos was what many would call a Dom, but he sure enjoyed taking cock, too. He just kept control while he did so, and that was sexier than anything Troy could think of just then.

Troy looked over at Will. "Where's Carlos?"

Will didn't look away from his laptop as he tapped at the keys. "He was expecting a call back from Glenn. I think he's on the porch again."

"Can't blame him. That sky is something to see." Troy shifted in the chair, his dick not willing to let him forget his thoughts from moments ago. He cleared his throat and Will stopped typing long enough to glance at him. Troy framed his package with his hands and rubbed his balls through his jeans. "You ever think about making a tape on purpose?"

Will wasn't slow, at all. He gasped a little, though, and his little nipples formed points that poked at his thin T-shirt. Someone else liked the idea, too.

"Do you think Carlos would?"

Wow. Will's cheeks were turning pink, his skin flushing up from the vee of his shirt. Troy hadn't seen him this turned on for a while. "Why not? He trusts us. It isn't like we'd put it on XTube or any of the other sites like that." Troy sat up and leant forward, elbows braced on his knees. The position wasn't exactly comfortable on his cock, but that just made him enjoy it more right then. "Imagine watching it while we're all fucking. Seeing what you look like while Carlos is pounding into you."

Will's cheeks went darker, and Troy was astounded, because Will never seemed to get embarrassed, but he was pretty sure that was what he was seeing then. "What's wrong, baby? What do you want?"

Will squirmed and Troy noted the bulge of his erection. Yeah, Will was definitely wanting.

"Tell me," Carlos said from the doorway, startling them

both. Troy and Will both jumped and Will squeaked right before he stood up, slapping a hand to his chest.

"Jesus, you scared the hell out of me!"

Will was just simply too adorable. Troy stood and got behind him, moving them both to do so. He held Will against him, cupping Will's denim-covered shaft in his palms. "How much did you hear?"

Carlos crossed his arms over his chest. "Enough to know we'll be needing the video camera and tripod."

"I can get it," Will exclaimed, already in motion. Troy held him in place as Carlos shook his head.

"Oh no. You are gonna tell me what had your face so red. I haven't seen you like that before, so spit it out." Carlos came over and stroked Will's cheek. "You know you can tell us anything. There's nothing you can ask for that'll turn us off or away."

Will lowered his eyes, giving Troy a pretty showing of his long lashes. "Would you fist me?"

Fisting, breathplay – Will was more adventurous than Troy would ever be.

Carlos looked at him, then back at Will. "Have you thought about that? Fantasising and reality –"

"I know," Will interrupted, "you've told me. But the breathplay was good, you know? I haven't come that hard in ages. I knew you wouldn't let me get hurt, and I wouldn't have laid there and let anyone hurt me, either. Still cranked my engine, big time. I promise if it's too much, I'll tell you."

Troy realised he'd been clenching his butt during that whole chat. He forced himself to relax. Will's cock was hard as diamond under his palms, and Troy could feel a bit of dampness, too, Will's eagerness leaking right out his slit.

"That's something we have to prepare for," Carlos warned. "It isn't gonna happen tonight, or tomorrow night. We need some better lube, and an enema kit, for starters."

"I can get them in Bozeman tomorrow." Will chortled then. "Aw, man, maybe I can have Drake pick up groceries while I run to a pharmacy. I don't want to freak him out."

Or make him feel worse than he probably did, Troy figured. "Just so it's out there, I don't want anyone's hand up my ass."

Will laughed again and Carlos nodded as he spoke. "Nope, didn't figure you would. Now, Will here, I was expectin' this from eventually."

Will fluttered his lashes and wiggled in Troy's arms. "Yeah, I am a wild man." He wiggled again, grinding against Troy. "And this wild man needs to be fucked."

"We can do that, sure enough," Carlos told him. Then he stared into Troy's eyes. "And after we both fuck you, Troy's gonna get it up again and lay down while I come all over his cock."

"Fuck," Troy whispered, his belly going tight and hot.

"That's the plan." Carlos tugged Will out of his arms and hefted him right on up over his shoulder in a fireman's hold. He slapped Will's ass hard, Will yelping and humping away. "We're gonna make sure we all get what we need." Carlos reached out and pinched one of Troy's nipples. Troy almost came on the spot. He didn't get to fuck Carlos' ass near often enough. Maybe if he weren't so eager to have Carlos fuck him...

Carlos flicked his nipple again and Troy surged forward, grabbing Carlos' nape to take a kiss he needed more than air just then. Carlos growled and bit at his lips, taking control of the kiss before Troy could any more than he had at first. Troy tasted blood on his tongue. He didn't know or care which of them it was from. Their kiss was harsh, a battle at times and Troy's surrender at others.

Soon Troy was stripping off his clothes while Carlos divested Will of his. He set Will right over his knees and began spanking Will's plump ass before Troy had finished getting naked.

Troy watched Will's skin darken with each spank. Will keened and rocked up, eagerly meeting each hit. Troy got his pants and underwear off then stepped in front of Will. He didn't even have to tell him to suck, Will just opened his mouth on a moan and took Troy's cock right on in.

Troy braced himself with a hand on Carlos' shoulder and one on Will's head. He thrust as soon as he knew Will could take him, and the wet, silky glide of Will's throat muscles almost spun him into orgasm.

Troy pulled his cock free and rubbed the wet length all over Will's face as Carlos kept up the blows to his backside. Will could take a lot more pain than Troy, although Will said it wasn't really pain, but a pleasure so intense it seared his insides.

Carlos landed one more smack, then he pulled Will up and flopped back on the bed, Will sprawled on top of him. "Fuck him," Carlos ordered, grabbing Will's ass and pulling it open.

Troy fetched the lube and poured it right into Will's crease. He tossed the tube aside and smeared the viscous stuff down to Will's hole. Two fingers in at once, and Will was humping against Carlos. Carlos let go of Will's ass and fisted his hands in Will's hair instead before kissing him.

Troy got on the bed, his knees framing Carlos and Will's thighs. He pulled Will's hips up then pressed his cock to Will's hole. "Take me," he said. He thrust, a hard, sharp drive that seated his length to the root in Will's welcoming ass.

Will made a garbled sound, back arching as Troy shoved in a little more. Will's butt was hot, literally hot from the spanking that had left it a deep shade of red. Troy knew that every time he drove his hips against that skin, Will really felt him.

He pounded into Will's ass, holding Will's lean hips and just going at it. The rhythmic milking of his cock by Will's inner walls told him just how much Will was enjoying the fucking.

Troy spread his legs a little more and dropped down over Carlos and Will, catching himself on one hand. He drove in deeper, harder, Carlos' hold on Will the only thing that kept Will from shooting forward.

"More," Will demanded, shouting it as if his life depended on Troy hearing him.

Troy nipped Will's nape, then the side of his head, catching Carlos' fingers, too. He was frantic with his need for release. Will was whimpering, raising that sweet ass of his up for every brutal thrust, and Troy was so close—

Carlos shoved fingers into Troy's mouth. He didn't know how many, only that he was stuffed, and it was erotic and something else, something that made him feel like his mouth was being used as a fuck hole. It blew his orgasm right out of his dick.

Troy shot and shot, Will's inner walls pulling the spunk out of him. He groaned and carefully pulled out before rolling onto his side, only to flop onto his back when pain radiated out from his ribs. Troy opened eyes he didn't remember closing just in time to see Carlos flip Will over and push his thick veiny cock into Will's hole.

Will howled and cum squirted from his dick. The glistening wetness on Will's belly told Troy Will had already come once, at least. Carlos pulled Will up onto his hands and knees and grabbed a handful of Will's hair. He fucked Will harder and rougher, pulling his head this way then that way, adding a slap to Will's ass every few thrusts.

Troy's cock began twitching to life again after several minutes of watching. Carlos never lost control, his expression stern but his dark eyes loving as he told Will how perfect and tight his ass was, how good it felt being in there after Troy lubed the way for him.

Speaking of lube, where'd I drop it? Carlos was going to be tighter even than Will since he didn't bottom much. Troy watched Carlos and Will a little longer, amazed at Carlos' stamina—and Will's too, but Carlos was really exerting a lot of energy with the way he was fucking Will. Troy saw when Carlos' balls pulled up, the sac wrinkling as he got ready to shoot.

Troy got the lube and returned to the bed just in time to watch Will come again. Carlos ground against his ass, the tendons in his neck standing out like they did when he was about to climax.

But Carlos didn't. He pulled that still-erect, glistening cock out of Will's ass then eased Will down onto his belly. "Sweetheart," Carlos murmured to Will, kissing his temple. Will hummed and Carlos turned his head to look at Troy.

"Get on your back, however's comfortable for you. I'm ready to get fucked."

Troy understood then why Carlos had held back. If he'd have come, there'd have been a waiting period before Troy could have fucked him. Everything went tense and tighter then a rich woman's purse strings in a recession when Carlos came. The foreplay to get him loosened up again was always fun, but Carlos had obviously wanted his orgasm to occur while Troy's dick was inside him.

Troy propped himself up against the headboard and Carlos took the lube from him. Carlos kicked off his jeans, having only pulled them down to fuck Will earlier. He took his shirt off too, then smirked at Troy and got up. Troy wasn't the only one to gasp when Carlos put his Stetson on. Carlos naked except for that hat was an awe-inspiring sight.

Carlos strolled to the bed, rolling his lean hips and making his dick tap his belly with each step. He stopped and turned his back to them and Troy knew they were going to get a show.

Sure enough, Carlos glanced over his shoulder at them as he pulled one ass cheek aside. Troy's mouth tingled seeing the whirl of his pucker framed by dark hair. "Can I—" He licked his lips.

"Me too," Will begged. "Please?"

Carlos backed up and bent at the waist. "I know you asked first," he said, looking at Troy, "but once I'm up on you, I ain't getting down until we're both fucked out."

"'Kay," was the best Troy could get out then because Will was pushing his face right in between Carlos' cheeks.

"Lick it, let me feel it, baby."

Troy reached for his own shaft and ringed the base with finger and thumb. He tilted his head and watched Will eat Carlos' ass. Sloppy, wet sounds filled the air, mixing with Troy's panted breaths and Carlos' orders and praise. By the time Carlos had Will stop, Will was jerking himself off.

Carlos got on the bed and straddled Troy's chest backwards, putting his ass right *there* where Troy could get to it. Troy clasped Carlos' thighs and went to town, tongue-fucking his wet, gaping hole.

Carlos was calling the shots. When he hissed louder than a balloon leaking air and started knee-walking away from Troy's face, Troy could have sung for joy. His dick was so hard it ached from his groin to his eyeballs. He heard the snap of the lube cap. Carlos shoved a hand between his cheeks, then he lined Troy's cock up and sank down on it so quickly Troy was overwhelmed with sensations. Carlos' ass was mind-boggling tight, and so hot it was almost too much. Troy bellowed and arched, his ribs and the pain there forgotten as pleasure suffused his body.

Carlos didn't give him time to adjust. He set a hard, fast ride, coming up until the underside of Troy's crown tugged at his rim before sliding down again.

"C'mere, Will," he heard Carlos say, then all he could do was pant and moan as Will got in front of Carlos. Will's back was to them both, and every time Carlos came up, an "Unh" sound left Will. Carlos didn't rise up as far, fucking Will again at the same time he rode Troy's dick.

Carlos sat down hard and pulled Will into his lap. Sharp, rapid thrust of his hips, and fierce constricting of his inner walls brought Troy to climax from one heartbeat to the next. He didn't feel the slow build up, the warming and pooling and anticipation. His release overpowered him, blacking his vision and leaving him voiceless as he shot his release into Carlos' ass.

When Troy came back to himself, his head feeling like someone had filled it with static and his body heavy with exhaustion, Will was on one side of him and Carlos on the other. That was good enough for him, and all he needed to know just then.

Chapter Thirteen

Will tucked his bag of goodies under the seat then went to meet Drake at the store. He felt bad leaving the man alone even for a while after he'd got tested, but Drake had assured him he'd be fine. The results for his HIV test wouldn't be in for up to three days. The test in the office had shown negative, but considering Drake's risk factors since his ex was positive—and had been for an unknown period of time—the nurse had recommended a more extensive test. Even an all-clear on it wasn't a sure thing, and Will found himself scared to believe that Drake was negative. And if he was scared to hope, how must Drake feel?

Will found him in the produce aisle. Drake had a smile for him, and it almost even reached Drake's eyes. "Get your errand taken care of?"

"Yeah, I did. Do you need me to get anything here?" Will wanted to ask Drake if he needed a hug.

"Nah, I'm done. Well." He plucked a fat red onion out of a bin. "Now I'm done. Bag this." Drake tossed him the onion and Will caught it. He put it in a bag while Drake wheeled the grocery cart to the registers. Will joined him and put the onion on the conveyor belt once they got close enough to it. They unloaded the basket and after they'd paid and were loaded up and heading home, Will decided to just ask.

"Are you feeling okay?" Well, that was a dumb question. "I mean, not okay, but—"

"I know what you mean," Drake said, saving Will from making a bigger fool of himself. "And I don't know about feeling okay, but I'm not feeling like I'll die tomorrow. That's how I felt when Rigo called me at first, and when he wouldn't answer me about how long he'd had HIV or when he'd become aware of having it, I just thought I was going to fall apart worse than I did. But here's what I've realised." Drake hitched one leg up as he turned to face Will.

"I can't change anything that's happened. If I have HIV, I have to accept that and do everything I can to take care of myself. No more selfish jerks for boyfriends, and I'm sure there's a million other lifestyle changes I'll have to make. There's a lot to take in, and today I'm okay. Tomorrow I might be a blubbering mess. Who knows. I want to keep as busy as I can though until I get the results back. Keep me from dwelling on it completely." Drake sighed then and settled into more of a slouch. "I bought more gloves, too. I've been wearing them ever since Rigo called."

Will hadn't noticed that at first, but a couple of mornings after, Carlos had mentioned it after they'd had dinner. "We appreciate you being honest and trusting us." He saw Drake shrug.

"I don't have anyone else, but you, Carlos and Troy are good people, and I try to be. I would have told you anyway."

Will's phone chimed and he plucked it from his pocket. A tap and he was talking to Carlos. "Hey, stud, you calling to tell me how much you miss me?"

"You know I do," Carlos said after chuckling. "But on top of that, I just heard from Glenn again. He told me last night he was expecting a call about Freddie Jr. Turns out he was moved to a hospital in Bozeman."

Will slowed the truck down. "You want me to go check on him?"

"Might make Troy happy to know how the kid was doing. Glenn said tell the front desk nurse he sent you. Someone he knows is handling the whole privacy issue. You shouldn't have any trouble getting in. Take Drake with you if you want."

"I'll leave that up to him." Will slowed even more. He checked for traffic, saw none, and made a U-turn. "Do you want to talk dirty to me before we hang up?"

"Now why would I want to have you sportin' wood with another man in the truck?" Carlos asked. "Be careful, call if you need me. Love you, Will."

Damn. Will went soft and gooey inside. "Love you too, cowboy."

Drake's exaggerated sigh was kind of cute. Will winked at him.

"I bet you hear it a lot from people who know about you, Carlos and Troy, but daaaamn, talk about hot. Depressing, too, because you each have two good men and I can't even snag one." Drake said it with a smile, so Will didn't think he was serious about the depressing part. "So, why are we going back to Bozeman? Are the cold foods in danger?"

"Seems nippy enough outside that they should be all right, don't you think?" Will asked. "There's an empty ice chest in the back seat we can use, too."

Drake craned his neck and rose up on his knee to peer over the headrest of his seat. "Huh. I didn't see that. I guess I should pay more attention."

"You had other things on your mind." And Will could have kicked himself for saying so. He rushed on, hoping to cover his faux pas. "You remember the young man whose father beat him up?"

"Yeah."

"That's who we're going to see. Should be weird because I don't know him and he's never met me, but Troy would like to know how he's doing. Fortunately we have a former FBI agent for a friend and he's cleared the way for me to get in to see Freddie."

About that time Will's phone buzzed, letting him know he had a text. He handed the phone to Drake. "Can you read that to me?"

"Sure." Drake took the phone. "It's the address for the hospital."

Will snorted. "Yeah, I guess that'd be handy to have. I didn't even think, just turned around and started driving back to town."

"I can type it into your nav app if you want."

"That'd be great."

It took him almost an hour to find the hospital thanks to a wreck on the highway and his nav's insistence on sending him searching for streets that didn't exist. Finally he parked in the lot. He and Drake loaded the cold foods into the cooler then locked the truck up, Drake having decided to come in with him.

The hospital was decent-sized, and clean enough as such things went. Will hated the smell of the place. It smelt like a hospital, as if the invisible battle between germs and cleaners actually had an odour, the same for all germs and cleaning products combined.

"I'm almost ready to believe that all hospitals use the same chemical-smelling air freshener," he groused before they reached the front desk.

"They do reek," Drake said faintly.

Will stopped and turned to his friend, giving Drake a solid once-over. The man looked pale and nervous. "Hey, maybe this isn't a good idea for you after all."

Drake shook himself, then rolled his shoulders. "No, no, it's fine. I can't be so…so moody."

"I would be." Will didn't even doubt it. "I would be a complete head case, even—" *Oh shit!*

"Even after the test in the office was negative," Drake finished for him. "It's okay, Will. I won't pretend it isn't happening, even if I wish it weren't. I keep thinking if I just hadn't let Rigo fuck me that last time…" He rubbed at his eyes then blinked. "Enough of that. I can't go there."

"Yeah, Carlos always says the what-ifs and could-haves should be avoided or they'll take over your mind." Will touched Drake's arm, just a pat to let him know he was touchable. Will had read a new article where a man who had HIV said the worst part was no one would touch him, and he didn't want Drake to feel that way. People needed touches, and hugs, and friendly pats.

At the front desk, a male nurse with a receding hairline

and a huge smile greeted them. Despite the whole vanishing hair thing, Will figured the man to be around his own age, maybe a few years older. He was friendlier than a lot of nurses Will had met.

"Hi. A friend of ours is in the hospital, and we were told—"

"Oh, I bet you two are here to see Freddie! Great!"

Will felt one of his eyebrows crawling up and quickly got himself under control. That was a lot of exuberance for anyone to have, and that was saying something coming from him.

"So my boss said to bring you straight back—like I know straight." The nurse giggled. "Anyway, Freddie's back this way. Chuckie—he's my boss—he used to work for the FBI. Not that he said so, but everyone knows everyone else's business around here. And gossip? Oh honeys, doctors out-gossip us nurses any day of the week, and we are constantly yammering about someone or another. There can be so much bad stuff at a hospital that we like to get our kicks where we can. And oh! I'm Landon, the one and only. There's not another like me in the world!"

Will would bet there wasn't. Two hyper blabbermouths like Landon would have to cause some kind of interstellar combustion, a chain of explosions from star to star and planet to planet—or just a complete desire to press the BOOM button for planet Earth. Anything to escape twice the talking and bounciness. Drake was wincing constantly, like each step was painful. Will totally understood that. Landon was just too much.

"Here's his room. Let me just peek in first and make sure he isn't peeing in the urinal jug or anything like that."

"What else 'like that' could there be?" Drake asked once Landon was in the room.

"No freakin' idea."

The door opened and Landon stuck his head out. "He's asleep. You can come in and see him. Maybe he'll wake up."

Landon flitted out and Will and Drake went in. Will

whispered, "Guess having to keep it down was too much of a challenge for Landon."

"S'why I faked being asleep."

Will squeaked in surprise, he couldn't help it. He looked at the form on the bed. Freddie was covered in bruises, and there were tubes and wires connected to him, reminding Will of a cyborg since he'd just read the best sci-fi book a day before.

"Sorry," Freddie slurred. Or was it Fred Jr? Will was going to confuse himself, so he just used the most effective method to find out and asked.

"Is it Fred, Fred Jr, or Freddie?"

"Anthony."

"Well, now I'm *really* fucking confused." Maybe they were in the wrong room. Landon had been flighty enough—*God, just think about having him as my nurse!* "I guess—"

"S'right room. Frederick Anthony Bell. No more Fred."

"FAB? Really? That's—"

"Anthony," Fred-Freddie-Anthony said. Will shoved the other two names into his mental garbage bin and told himself to call the kid Anthony like he asked.

"Okay, well, Anthony, I'm—"

"I know."

Will was going to get irked quickly if he got interrupted again. "You know what?"

"Who you are. Not him," Anthony gestured towards Drake.

"I'm Will," Will got out then he put a hand on Drake's shoulder. "This is Drake. He's a friend, and our cook out at the Mossy G."

Anthony swallowed. His throat clicked and Will figured since he didn't have any tubes in his mouth, he could have a drink. He spotted the plastic pitcher and cup beside the bed. "Do you want a drink?"

"Please."

Anthony said it so pitifully that Will's chest ached for the kid. He went to the stand and poured some water in the cup. A straw was laid out so Will put it in the cup then carefully held the straw to Anthony's lips. This close, he could see the kid's eyes were a deep green, the colour made deeper, he'd bet, by all the bruising. Anthony's nose had a hook to it, like it'd been broken once or twice, but there was no brace or even a bandage on it now so Will assumed it wasn't damaged beyond some swelling. Anthony sipped at the water. When he was done he pushed the straw away with his tongue. During the entire time, he hadn't looked away from Will. It was creepy.

"You called me."

Will jerked back and almost dropped the cup. There was that creepy thing again. Anthony looked like he was...was crushing on Will. *Shit.*

Anthony's eyes gleamed. "It was you, I know it was. You—"

There was no need to let the kid get the wrong idea. *Or more of a wrong idea, whatever.* "I was calling because Troy was afraid you'd been seriously hurt, and he was right." Will cocked his head, one question bouncing around insistently inside his head. "How did you even know it was me? I've never talked to you in person. I wouldn't have thought you'd know what my voice sounded like."

Guilt, that was what Will saw in the kid's expression. Will barely kept from glaring, suspicion prickling his spine. "Tell me," he demanded, trying his best to sound like Carlos.

Anthony rolled his head away and closed his eyes. "Heard you before. I didn't mean to cause trouble. At first I was mad and it helped me not to do something stupid. More stupid, like kill myself."

"Nothing's ever that bad," Will snapped, his temper flitting free for a moment before he got it under control again. He had a bad feeling that he knew what Anthony *wasn't* saying. "You're the one who did it. You sprayed that crap all over the barns, the sheds and—"

"I'm sorry. I'm so, so sorry." Anthony started to sob. Will was torn between bitching the kid out and giving him a hug. Considering the way Anthony had been eyeing him minutes ago, Will settled for talking.

"Look, I understand what you've been through."

Anthony choked on a denial, but Will shut him down. "I do. I have the scars to prove it, inside and out. I didn't let it ruin me, though—"

"You're just a better man than me," Anthony said bitterly.

"If you interrupt me again, you'll be wearing the rest of the ice water that's in the pitcher," Will warned, lifting the container. Drake laughed behind him and Will gave him a look, daring him to doubt him.

Drake held up both hands. "I believe you."

Anthony didn't say a word and Will set the pitcher down again. "Your father might have shaped your world until now, but from this moment on, everything you do is on your head. You can't blame him for tagging other people's property with bad artwork. You can't destroy other people's stuff to make yourself feel good. You have to decide if you want to get better, get past *your* past, or if you're going to keep reliving it. If, someday, you'll have a son who you abuse."

"No," Anthony cried out, turning back to Will. "I won't! Haven't you figured it out? I'm gay! I love you!"

Oh. Oh, not good, not good at all. Will resisted looking at Drake as Anthony kept talking. Will really wished he'd just shut up.

"I saw you, the first day you showed up at the ranch. I didn't think anyone would ever buy it, see? It was there and I was so angry. I would… I would go out there and beat on whatever, tear things up. Spray my shitty drawings onto the buildings."

Will cringed. "Sorry about that. I was probably, uh, harsh."

Anthony glared. "I suck, I know. What we want and what we have, they aren't always the same, right?"

Will didn't answer. He had what he wanted, needed, in Carlos and Troy.

"For most of us, anyway." Anthony looked at Drake. "I bet you don't have what you want either."

Drake stepped forward, and for the first time, Will saw the fury in his friend's eyes. "I don't have what I want? You know what? I get that your situation was shitty, man, okay? I get it. But you're alive, and you can start over and quit being your daddy's punching bag."

"It's not that easy—" Anthony started.

"Yes, it is," Drake yelled before taking a steadying breath.

Landon zipped into the room, eyes huge in his face. "Is there a problem in here?"

"No problem," Will told him, "they're discussing politics. Never a good subject unless you're on the same side."

Landon's mouth curved into an O. "He's a Republican? Freddie, really?"

"No."

"Just a difference of opinion on Democrats versus libertarians," Will offered, smiling at Landon. "We're all sort of on the same page, just not on the same paragraph."

"Okay, but no more yelling or out you go." Landon left and Drake went right back to lecturing Anthony.

"It's as easy as deciding it's time for you to be an adult and live the kind of life you want to live. Other people might have screwed you over, maybe even hurt you permanently or..." Drake looked up at the ceiling, blinking rapidly as he did so. "Or someone you thought you could trust might have put you at risk and not given a shit. Whatever it is, you get to decide what comes next. *You.* And for the record, Will is happy with Troy and Carlos. No one will break them up."

"Both?" Anthony croaked.

Will rolled his eyes. "Leave it to him to comment on that part only."

"There's nothing wrong with it," Drake said, sounding rather huffy. "They love each other and treat each other better than any couple I've seen. If I could be half as loved by someone, I'd count myself lucky. Anyone who wants to judge them should get their head out of their prudish ass."

Will was over talking about his personal life. It just wasn't anyone else's business. "What happens between me and my husbands is our business, Anthony. We are, however, going to have to talk to you about what you've done. You've cost us a lot of money and man hours. Do you have *any* idea how much I fucking hate painting?"

"I just wanted you to come in the store. It was the other guy, Troy though. Never you. Then you called—"

"And I told you why I did. Look." Will rubbed his forehead, feeling a headache start up right between his eyebrows. "I'm not going to keep telling you. This is the last time. I am happy, beyond happy, with Carlos and Troy. There is no hope for anything from me but maybe friendship—" Will pinned Anthony with a guarded look. "Even that's not guaranteed. It depends on what kind of person you choose to be, because I don't do toxic relationships of any sort. Not with friends, not with family, no one. Do you understand everything I just said?"

"Yes," Anthony rasped. Tears leaked down his cheeks, but he didn't seem to notice. "I'm a fuck-up. I get it."

"No, you don't." Will hoped Troy didn't take it too hard when Will had to tell him the truth about Freddie-Anthony. "You don't get it at all, but I guess there's still hope." His mood was down around his ankles, but Will tried to get past it. Troy would want some other answers. "How bad are your injuries? I don't see a cast anywhere."

Anthony made a sound that might have been a laugh—or a sob. "Nothing broke. Bruised ribs, concussion, lost some teeth. Pissing blood. Bruising inside me. I'll live." Anthony looked at him. "And when I get out of here, I'll come to the Mossy Glenn and take whatever punishment your husbands want to give me. For the destruction of property and for wanting to fuck you."

Will was going to throttle the kid. He had to walk away. "You do that." Will didn't look back as they left.

In the hallway, Drake stopped him, holding Will's wrist.

"You know he's figuring Carlos and Troy are going to beat the shit out of him, like his daddy did. He figures he's got it coming, and that's why he tried to make sure you were pissed off enough to rile up the other two with that comment about fucking you."

"Aw, damn." Will never did stay angry at anyone long. "Shit. I should have known that. Sounds like something I'd have done."

Drake leered. "Yeah, but you've had the love of two good men to chase off that part of you, so you already forgot about some of it. That's the way it should be. Love should heal all, conquer all—you know, mushy stuff like that."

"It does," Will said, realising just how true it was. "It really does. Now let's go home."

Chapter Fourteen

Carlos watched Troy hammering away at the porch railing on the second bunkhouse. He'd been in an off mood ever since Will had come back from Bozeman and told them about Fred – Anthony. Carlos wasn't mad, as such. He kind of understood the kid's need to get out the anger, and at least Anthony hadn't hurt anyone else, he'd just cost them money and made them waste time painting and repairing the place. Carlos also understood his crush on Will. He didn't begrudge the kid the desire to fuck Will, either, but he'd never let Anthony touch Will. Hell, Will wouldn't let Anthony touch him.

Troy set the hammer down and wiped sweat off his brow before looking up at Carlos. "I know. I've been in a funk. I just don't get how I misjudged Fred Jr so badly."

"Anthony," Carlos corrected. "No reason to be stubborn about his name."

Troy scowled and picked the hammer up. He stuck it back in his tool belt. "I know. I'm a dick."

"No, you're pissed. I get that, but I also get that Anthony's primary and first example on how to be a man was his father. I get that he lived in a town where most people had to know what was going on yet no one interfered. I get that he'd be a mess, and you'd feel tricked 'cause you got a tender heart and were worried for the kid." Carlos came over and tipped Troy's head up. "There's nothing wrong with caring about anyone, Troy. Most people ain't all good or all bad, and we've all done things we're ashamed of. I can remember stealing candy from the corner gas station when I was a teenager. We were poor, but I wasn't starving.

I just wanted what I wanted, and I knew it wasn't right. That's not so different from what Anthony's done."

"It's a lot different," Troy argued. "You took a piece of candy. We're talking thousands of dollars in destruction of property when we first got here, then probably thousands more in paint and labour and fuckin' surveillance cameras!"

Carlos hated confessing, but he had to. "I stole more than a piece of candy, Troy." Carlos looked towards the porch and saw Will coming their way. He waited until Will was with them to go on. It was humiliating and he'd rather just do it once.

"I was telling Troy that Anthony ain't hopeless and it ain't wrong to care about someone even if they do bad shit. I used to steal candy when I was fourteen or so. Stole beer, too, and cigarettes. I don't know if I'd have stopped if my Mama hadn't figured it out and took a belt to my ass. Even at fourteen, I wasn't dumb enough to sass my Mama. Lord, she took the skin off my rump. That was the end of my thieving, but you know, I still wanted to steal. Took a while to get past that. I missed the thrill of it more than I missed the shit I took."

"Few people are all good or all bad. I don't want to meet either type."

Carlos looked at Will. Will shrugged. "What? The evil ones are psycho killer kinds, right? And the all good, that'd be, like, God and Jesus and I really don't want to meet them yet, either."

"Smartass." Carlos rubbed Will's bottom then tucked his hand into one of Will's back pockets. "Didn't you ever do anything bad, Troy?"

Troy sighed noisily enough to spook the pretty new Quarter Horse in the corral. "Sorry, Quince," he called to the horse as she skittered away. "Shit. Yes." He narrowed his eyes. "Is this confession time or something?"

"Sure. I shouldn't be the only one baring his criminal past."

"You might be," Will teased. "I'm a good boy."

"Man," Troy and Carlos said.

"That too."

Troy took the hammer out and rolled it in his hands. "Okay. I've tried most every kind of drug there was up until six or seven years ago. Wasn't hooked on any, just wanted to see what they did. And I might have burned an ex's entire album collection."

"Might have?" Carlos asked.

"That's mean," Will said at the same time. "I like it."

"I'm glad we have CDs," Carlos countered.

"They burn," his men informed him.

Carlos arched a brow at Will.

"Oh, fine," Will grumbled. "You know I've hacked into some government places that could have gotten me put in prison for a long time."

Carlos felt a fissure of unease come to life in him. Troy looked like he'd been poleaxed. Carlos asked, "Will, can they still arrest you? That's not something the government is likely to brush off if they figure out who did it."

"They won't." Will sounded very, very certain of that. "Any trail they find will lead to my sister. She's almost as good at hacking as I am. I used to feel bad about that, but she hurt me, many times." Will shrugged. "Does it make me a horrible person that I don't feel bad? I don't think it does. I hacked into those places because my dad made me. I haven't done anything like that since before I disowned all of them."

"You aren't a bad person."

"Not at all," Troy added. "And I'm glad you disowned your father and sibs. They weren't meant to have someone as wonderful as you in their lives."

"Aw, you're so sweet!" Will took the hammer out of Troy's hand and put it back in his tool belt. "You deserve a reward. Like for me to blow you."

Carlos needed to step in before Will ended up blowing Troy out in broad daylight. "Why don't you hold off on that?"

Will looked shocked. "Why? I wasn't going to do it here."

"Because I have plans for tonight that involve all of us and a video camera."

Will's eyes were almost as huge as Troy's, and both of them were sporting semis. Carlos grinned. "Save those. We're gonna want to have as many cum shots as possible."

"Oh my God! Cum shots!" Will squealed and clapped his hands together. "Yes!"

"Lunch is ready," Drake shouted from the porch. "Come get it before I eat it all myself!"

Will took off at a run, laughing like he'd never had a care in the world. Carlos and Troy followed more sedately. "You know his birthday's coming up next week."

"Yep, on the twentieth," Troy said. "I was thinking we should get him—"

"Sh, we'll talk later. I don't know how the sound is on these cameras he's got running out here." Carlos looked at one and waved. "Give him something to giggle over later."

Inside the house, they sat at the kitchen table. Carlos cut into his steak and moaned when he put it in his mouth. "Drake, you can't ever quit. No vacation either," he growled teasingly.

"Funny guy." Drake sat and cut his entire steak up into little bites before he began to eat. Carlos, Will and Troy were all but done by then. Drake swallowed a mouthful and set his silverware down.

Unease pricked at Carlos. Troy and Will felt it too, both of them giving him worried looks. Today was the day Drake was supposed to hear back from the clinic. Carlos believed in ripping the bandage off quick, but this was Drake's wound, not his.

"It was negative," Drake whispered, and no sooner had he said it than tears poured from his eyes. Will let out a whoop and tackled Drake for a hug. Troy was a little more reserved, patting Drake's arm and murmuring congratulations. Drake shook them off after a minute. "It doesn't mean I'm okay. I have to be tested again. It's only been three months since I left Rigo. Until we know for sure he didn't infect me, I'm afraid to celebrate."

Carlos stood. "Well, when you're ready to celebrate, you let us know. We'll take you to Bozeman and go dancing." Drake might not feel like he could hope yet, but Carlos did. He'd come to see Drake as a friend. "For now, why don't you get outside after you eat, and mark off where you want that garden you were talking about. We'll clean up in here."

Carlos hadn't seen Drake smile like that since before he'd got that phone call from Rigo. It was pretty cool to have friends.

* * * *

Will came out of the bathroom clean inside and out. Carlos directed him to the bed, where he'd laid down a couple of old blankets. "Hands and knees, baby. I want at that ass." Carlos pointed at the video camera, letting Will know it was on.

Will sauntered, rolling his hips and looking like sex on legs. He got on the bed, crawling with that pert ass up, flashing his pucker every chance he got. Troy came into the bedroom and Carlos let him stand there and watch until Will got in position. Then he turned to Troy. "Get in front of the camera, but don't block the view of Will. I want you to strip, slowly. Once you get naked, you start stroking that cock of yours and playing with your tits. Should keep you busy while I get undressed."

"Okay." Troy moved confidently into place. He set his phone down on the dresser and after tapping some buttons on it, music began to play. Troy smiled wickedly and began swaying, giving him and Will a show.

"Yeah, take it off," Will called out. "Show us that divine cock of yours."

Troy tipped his head back and ran his hands up and down his body. Carlos decided he was going to really have to fight for his self-control tonight. He moved back, wanting Will to watch Troy, and Troy to keep doing what he was doing.

Carlos quickly took his clothes off, watching his men when he could. He didn't worry if he missed a little bit, they'd have the video to watch. He slid his chaps on, feeling only a little ridiculous. Will and Troy always loved him in the chaps, along with his hat. Carlos put it on, too, then when Troy was beautifully nude and working his cock and tits, Will watching him and practically drooling, Carlos barked a command.

"That's enough. Get on the bed, on your back. Will's going to move until he's on his hands and knees above you."

"Holy shit, Carlos. You're so fucking sexy," Troy grated out, hands stilling on his body. Will just whimpered and started coming his way.

Carlos pointed at him. "What'd I tell you?" Will smirked and Carlos knew what he wanted, but it wasn't happening tonight. He wanted all of Will's sensation coming from Carlos' hand inside his ass, not from him smacking the outside of it.

"Will," Carlos rumbled.

Will stopped and frowned as Troy laid down.

"I want everything you're feeling coming from this"—Carlos held up his hand—"inside of you. I don't want you feeling the burn of a spanking on your skin."

"Okay," Will agreed eagerly. He crawled back and positioned himself over Troy.

Carlos took the large bottle of lube out from under the bed where he'd set it earlier. He took the bowl out from there as well and removed the hand towels from inside it.

"Kiss," he told Will and Troy. Damn it, he should have started out kissing them both. Well, he didn't have to add to his mistake. Carlos set the supplies on the bed and got to where he could join in the kissing. It was good, his and Troy's and Will's tongues twining, them sucking and nibbling at each other's lips. "Love you both," he told them as he moved back towards the foot of the bed. "Keep kissing."

Carlos pushed Troy's legs up until he had his feet close to his ass. His knees pushed against the back of Will's legs and that was good, giving Will more support. Carlos rubbed over Troy's hole with his left hand and Will's with his right. Both men moaned for him. He pushed his thumbs in, rubbing that guardian muscle over and over again. When he had it loosened, Carlos stopped long enough to pour the lube into the bowl.

He licked Will's ass hole, wetting it with his tongue while he went back to thumbing Troy's. When he had both of them moaning, Carlos dipped his hands in the bowl. Troy wouldn't need nearly as much lube since he wasn't going to be fisted, but it was easier just to dunk both hands.

"You ready for this, Will?"

"Yes," Will hissed. "Red, smack the bed, I'm ready!"

At least he was thinking, even if he did sound a little sarcastic.

"Troy, you want my fingers?"

Troy looked at Carlos, then at Will. "I want Will to fuck me."

"Really?" Will's voice came out so high-pitched it would have made dogs howl. "*Really?*"

"Yeah, really," Troy told him. "And if that's something you wanted to do regularly, you could have said."

Will cleared his throat then coughed, and still squeaked when he talked. "I don't know about regularly, but I'd love to fuck you now."

"Let me get Troy stretched for you," Carlos said, rearranging how he'd planned to do things. He wanted Troy to get the fucking he needed, and for Will to be able to give it to him. He used his slick fingers to stretch Troy's hole, then he set the bowl of lube on the floor and moved to the side. "Come on, Will. He's needing."

"I am," Troy panted. "Fuck, I need so bad, baby."

Will hooked his arms under Troy's knees and raised his ass up. "I'll take care of you. I might have to fuck you twice, because I gotta tell you, I'm already close."

"In me," Troy begged.

Will held his breath, his face a mask of concentration. Carlos lined his dick up for him, then Will pushed in. "Ungh, shit shit shit! So tight—" He shuddered as he bottomed out. "Why don't I do this often?"

"I dunno, but fuck me already."

Will let the obvious joke go, a sure sign that he was already barrelling towards orgasm. He pulled back and thrust into Troy's ass again.

"Stop treating me like you'll break me," Troy snarled.

"You like it easy," Will snarled right back. He added a hard jab of his hips and Troy scrabbled to grab his arms.

Carlos considered having Will suck him while Will fucked Troy, but he tossed the idea. Watching was too good, and he could wait.

"Easy my ass. Fuck. Me."

Will pinched Troy's nipple, got a shout for it, too. "I'm fucking you," he reminded Troy.

"Doesn't matter, when Carlos is on my cock he's still driving."

"Yeah," Will said, grimacing. "You got a point."

There was no more talking then, just the sounds of flesh slapping flesh, the slick sounds of penetration. Grunts and moans rang out constantly, and Will fucked Troy with rapid stabs, probably not deep, but hard.

Troy tossed his head and reached for his cock then spoke for the first time in several minutes. "Give it to me, now!"

Will humped a half dozen more times, then he wailed as he stilled, only his buttocks trembling as he came.

Troy's moan was a long, low one that lasted as long as his climax. He gasped for air after, his mouth open and eyes closed. "God. Damn," he said later, "I think I'm fucked out already."

"Doubt it." Carlos traced over where Will's dick was still buried in Troy's hole and Troy shivered, cum seeping out. "I bet you can come again with my fingers in you."

"I know I can." Will pulled out slowly and his cock was

half-hard, either not having gone soft yet or else already perking back up. Will was something else. "I'm ready."

Carlos bet he was. "Get beside Troy and tuck your knees under you. You'll need to rise up and spread eventually, but for now that's how I want to start." Carlos made a rolling motion with his fingers. "You too, Troy, unless it hurts you."

"I'm fine. I haven't had more than a twinge for a day or two now."

"Look at you two," Carlos murmured, stroking both of his men's flanks. "Side by side, ain't a hotter sight in this world. Troy, your hole is open and wet, just waiting for something to fill it."

Carlos got the bowl from the floor and coated his hands again. He wasted no time pushing two fingers into each man. Troy was stretched enough to take it, and Will liked that pinch.

"Yes, fuckin' yes." Troy arched and pushed his butt up just like Will did.

"More," Will begged. "Please, Carlos. Please fill me up."

Carlos twisted his fingers inside Troy and Will. He brushed over Troy's prostate first, and Troy moaned. Will whimpered and begged and Carlos added a third digit.

"Mm, that's nice," Will told him. "Can't wait to feel all of your hand in me."

"Stop pushing me, baby," Carlos warned him. He slipped a third finger inside Troy's ass and Troy tensed for a moment, those silky walls rippling. "Okay, Troy?"

"Yeah, it's just a lot after being fucked."

Carlos pulled back at the same time he pushed his other fingers deeper into Will, touching his gland. "Too much? I can stop."

"No!" both men shouted.

"I meant for Troy."

"Oh thank God," Will rasped.

"No, don't stop, but I don't think I can take more."

Carlos thought that was probably accurate. He was proud

of Troy for knowing his limits. "Well, let's see if I can blow your mind."

Gently he began finger-fucking Troy while he stopped fingering Will long enough to dip his hand in lube again. This time he sank it in past his wrist before returning to push four fingers in Will's hole.

"Uhn, uhn." Will rocked back, trying to fuck himself on Carlos' fingers.

"Quit that, Will. I won't have you hurting yourself. You either let me do the fucking or this stops." It wasn't that he didn't trust Will, it was that Will tended to get lost in sensations, and it was Carlos' job at those times to make sure Will was safe. "Come up a bit and spread your knees apart."

Once Will had done as he was told, Carlos went to fucking him in counter-rhythm to his strokes in Troy. Troy's cock had plumped back up and he was rubbing it, working that tip. Carlos wished he had another pair of hands, but he didn't so all he could do was watch.

When Will's hole was good and loose, Carlos' fingers gliding in and out easily, he tucked his thumb and added into the mix. Will shook for him, mewling needily. Troy's ass constricted around Carlos' fingers on the next stroke, Will's voice breaking on a wordless yell as he came. Carlos murmured soothingly and took his fingers out as Will dug his heels into the bed.

Then Carlos concentrated on pushing into Will's hole over and over, stretching that rim. "Okay, Will?"

Will moaned for him and arched his back. Troy rolled onto his side then scooted down. He reached under Will and fisted his cock just as Carlos prepared to fist Will's ass.

"You still want to take my hand?"

"Please," Will whined.

"All right, just try to relax back here." He rotated his hand, Will's ring giving easily. "I'm going to put my whole hand in now, then you're going to be very, very still while I make a fist and start fucking you."

Will's answer was incoherent, but he nodded his head.

"His dick is harder than I've ever felt it," Troy said. "He's ready and wantin'."

Carlos pulled out, re-dipped his hand and wrist, then tucked his thumb and slowly but steadily pushed his fist into Will's ass. Will's pucker went white around his knuckles, and Carlos asked if Will wanted to stop. Will's cry of 'No' had him turning his hand. It slid right on in, and Carlos' cock wept with need as those slick tight walls contracted around his hand.

He curled it into a fist, his knuckles grazing Will's gland. Gentle pumps first, not going too deep. Will started babbling, rolling his head from side to side.

Troy raised up and looked at Carlos' fist going in and out of Will's ass. "Fuck!"

Carlos couldn't even speak for once, his throat constricted with emotion at Will's trust. He leant forward and sucked a mark-up on one butt cheek. He kept fucking Will while he did it, until Will shrieked like the ecstasy was too intense. His ass clamped down around Carlos' hand and Troy panted out that Will had come.

As if Carlos couldn't tell, but he got it. This was new and scary and fucking spine-meltingly good.

"We've got you," Carlos said, again and again until Will came down from the intense climax. "Now you have to work with me. It ain't gonna feel as good coming out as it did going in."

"Maybe I can help." Troy moved up again and started kissing Will. After a minute or two, his inner muscles relaxed and Carlos carefully pulled his hand out.

As soon as he did, he set the bowl on the floor and shot up to cuddle Will between him and Troy. "How do you feel, baby?"

"Used. So fucking good."

Carlos smiled and grasped his own cock. He needed to come now that he'd taken care of his men. "That's how you should feel."

"Need a hand?" Troy offered, reaching around Will and unerringly finding Carlos' cock. Carlos left off jerking himself and let Troy do it. It always felt better when Troy or Will pulled him off.

Carlos fucked Troy's hand with none of his usual finesse. Need drove him to a frenzy, and he couldn't even breathe as he came.

They'd have to get up and get clean this time around, but Carlos was a little too boneless to move just then. "Give me ten minutes, then we've got a date with the shower."

Will snickered. "For once, I don't think I'll be able to get it up again by then."

Looked like Carlos had done them all pretty damned good.

Ropes and Dreams

Excerpt

Chapter One

"Oh, no. Crap!" Drake Cuttington squatted and picked up Buddy. The puppy squirmed and whined, all the while trying to lick Drake to death. "No, no. Bad Buddy." Buddy yipped and wagged his tail, the solid thump of that appendage landing against Drake's ribs repeatedly. "Jesus, when you're full grown, that tail's gonna be a rib-breaker. What kind of dog are you?" Buddy had spots, but he sure wasn't a Dalmatian. Carlos had said the pups came from a shelter, so likely they were some kind of mix.

Buddy stretched his little head up and licked Drake's chin. Drake's irritation at having to clean up puppy pee lessened a great deal with that wet, warm show of affection. Still, there had to be rules.

"No doing that in the house, and especially not in my kitchen," he told the puppy. "You definitely need some training." Drake almost groaned at that. What did he know about puppies? He'd never been allowed to have a pet, not when he was a kid, and not when he'd hooked up with any of his exes. Honestly, he'd not been in a good place where he could have a pet since he'd left home at eighteen.

"You're gonna need shots and all kinds of stuff," he muttered, thoughts racing as he imagined lists to be made and subjects to Google. He really didn't know crap about puppies, babies, kittens or any other small, dependent-on-him life forms. Buddy whimpered and licked him right over the lips as he was mumbling to himself.

Drake sputtered and held Buddy away from him as he decided whether or not to be grossed out. "Well, dang it." Wow, he totally understood the saying about 'puppy-dog eyes' now. That had to be what Buddy was doing to him with those big brown eyes. Drake tried to hold out and be firm or whatever, but he caved and cuddled Buddy to his chest. "I'm so screwed. You're gonna be spoilt as all get-out. But you still can't use the house as your toilet, sweetie."

Drake rubbed the silky spot behind Buddy's ears. "Whoa, that's an addictive feeling. So soft. No wonder that crazy chick wanted a puppy coat."

Buddy rolled those big eyes up at him and Drake winced. "I didn't mean she was right, just that, uh, that a chinchilla's got nothing on this." He rubbed a little harder. Buddy made a sound that could only be called a groan and closed his eyes. "Rotten. You're gonna be rotten."

Drake petted him a few minutes longer, then he had to clean up the mess because it was just gross. Tucking Buddy under one arm snugly, Drake went and got the Swiffer out. "Thank God for this thing," he muttered as he took it back over to the wet spot. In short order, he had the puddle cleaned up. He put the Swiffer out on the porch, reminding himself to clean it later. "Now, there's got to be puppy supplies. I'd ask Carlos, Troy or Will but I'm pretty sure they don't want to be disturbed."

Though they did have three puppies with them as well.

Drake snickered at the idea of the three men trying to get their freak on with yapping, fluid-leaking puppies nipping at them. The puppies, all gifts for Will's birthday, were sure to be giving the men grief.

Although, thinking about it, Drake didn't hear any yapping or cursing. "Huh." Well, who knows? Maybe Carlos is a puppy whisperer or something and he got the other three to sleep so he could play with his guys. Whatever the deal, Drake only needed to worry about Buddy for now.

To that end, he went in search of puppy food. He knew his employers well enough to feel confident that they hadn't just brought puppies and no supplies. It was with a sigh of relief that he found food and bowls in the washroom, along with what looked like four cages.

Drake frowned at them. Were those to lock the pups up in? "Have to be. I don't think Carlos and his guys are into puppy play." Drake's face heated and he glanced around, but nobody was around other than him and Buddy. He looked at the cages again. They were black and made of thin strips of wire. Plastic trays were in the bottom of them. He didn't think he wanted to put Buddy in one. It seemed kind of cruel. Still, he'd do some reading, because Carlos wasn't a cruel man, so he probably knew something about puppies and cages that Drake didn't.

Drake took a blue bowl and set it on the floor. He put Buddy down, too, and the puppy ran right to the bowl. "Just a sec, sweetie." He chuckled at Buddy then went to the bag of dog food. It was open, and a shiny silver scoop was in it. The food itself reeked. Drake barely kept from gagging as he took some food out for Buddy. "Man, I am gonna have to look up dog food recipes. Surely there's something I can make that won't smell like stinky feet."

Buddy didn't seem to mind the smell, diving into the kibble with an enthusiasm that Drake envied. He wanted to be that happy and appreciative of anything.

Drake used another bowl to get Buddy some water. If the puppy needed milk, Drake would deal with that later. He watched Buddy eat for another moment before he noticed a turquoise collar and leash laid out on the dryer. Hoping those were Buddy's, he took them and examined them, shivering as soon as he touched them.

"Leather," he murmured. It was stupid, but just feeling the smooth, cool material, Drake's nipples ached and his cock twitched. He'd always loved leather, the look of it, the scent. Was it his imagination, or was the washroom now smelling slightly of leather? Drake sniffed and almost moaned. He fiddled with the buckle of the collar then stopped himself. Something was percolating in his brain and he didn't really want to go there, especially since he was never going to have sex again. Possibly not even with himself.

Okay, he didn't have that kind of self-control, but masturbation was all he was going to do for relief from now on. His scare with HIV was still riding on his shoulders. Drake realised then that, for the first time since his ex Rigo had called and told him he'd tested positive for HIV, he had managed not to think about the fear he'd been dealing with for over a week now.

Drake's tests had come back negative so far, but he was so afraid to hope they'd keep on being negative. He was even more afraid to think they wouldn't. HIV wasn't the death sentence it used to be, but it was still nothing to treat lightly, and people were still dying because of it.

Buddy's loud slurps and the skittering of his nails on the cement washroom floor snapped Drake out of his brooding. He had just enough time to shout "No!" then there was water all over, including on him. "Buddy," Drake whined, looking at his wet pants legs and the spreading water on the floor. Buddy sat and wiggled his little butt as he wagged his tail. Of course he sat in the water, and his tail slung droplets of it, too.

The back door squeaked as it was opened and Drake turned just enough to see Saul 'Salt' Johnson step into the room. "Got a problem there, Drake?"

Salt always looked at Drake in a way that made him think Salt might be interested in him, but Drake just wasn't up to going there with anyone. Drake faced his adorable, messy puppy again. "I have to bake two cakes for Will's birthday, and make y'all lunch and dinner. I don't know what to do with Buddy."

Salt came farther into the room. "Buddy, huh? He's a cute little bugger, ain't he? Looks like he's part Aussie and part heeler, maybe."

"Part Aussie?" Drake asked, peering at Salt, and trying not to let it show that he thought the guy must be off his rocker. There was no way Buddy had come from Australia, and how would Salt know if he had?

Salt just grinned and winked at him, sending something like panic skittering through Drake. "Well now, I don't rightly know where he comes from, but I'd think it's in the US. I meant he's probably part Australian Shepherd. Good dogs, pretty, too. Easy to train and energetic."

"Energetic's an understatement," Drake muttered as Buddy leapt up and started barking. "He's— Is he barking at the water?" Buddy bounced and slapped his paws down, sending a shower of sprinkles out.

"Yup, looks like," Salt agreed. "Want me to take him out for a walk? I can get him outta your hair for a while, let you get some cooking done."

Drake bit his bottom lip, debating. He wanted Buddy to love him best, did that make him petty? Then again, he wouldn't be able to keep Buddy if he lost his job and was homeless.

"That his leash and collar you're holding onto?"

Drake remembered the leather in his hands and despite his best effort not to, he blushed. "Er, yeah. I was"—getting turned on by it—"waiting for him to get done eating and drinking so I could put it on. Now he's all wet."

"That he is." Salt came over to where Buddy was splashing and having entirely too much fun spreading the water all over. He bent and picked up the puppy. Buddy looked tiny in Salt's hands. Drake looked away, not wanting Salt to think he was interested. Salt was probably a good guy and all, but Drake simply had never been attracted to guys so much older than himself. And, he admitted silently, he always dated jerks. Always. That was another reason for his intended celibacy.

"Looks like he's got a crate, too. That's good. Puppies like feeling safe, and they're pack animals. Those kennels become like a den for 'em once the dogs get used to them."

Drake glanced at Salt. "They aren't cruel? Like, locking the poor dogs in jail or whatever?" He felt like a fool for asking, but reminded himself he wasn't out to impress Salt. Besides which, Buddy was his. "I don't want him to hate me."

Salt gave a crooked grin and rubbed Buddy's belly. "Aw, nah. He won't. He'll try to guilt ya out of it, but it's better to put them in there than let 'em tear stuff up. Lots of dogs end up being dumped because their owners don't bother training 'em, but just like a kid, they gotta be taught how to behave. It's best to do that with love, not force."

"Okay." That was a lot to think about. Drake would deal with it later, because he just had to know something. "But—I just got him. Is he going to think he's yours if you take him now?"

"He'll figure out he's your little boy in no time," Salt assured him.

More books from Bailey Bradford

When Gabriel Staley rescues a magnificent black wolf, he has no idea that destiny has just turned up the heat.

Sometimes all it takes is a subtle breeze to shift the winds of fate.

Chance Galloway thinks walking into the Xxchange might just be the biggest mistake he's ever made

A run through the woods turned anything but typical when Levi found the one thing he never expected to find.

About the Author

Bailey Bradford

A native Texan, Bailey spends her days spinning stories around in her head, which has contributed to more than one incident of tripping over her own feet. Evenings are reserved for pounding away at the keyboard, as are early morning hours. Sleep? Doesn't happen much. Writing is too much fun, and there are too many characters bouncing about, tapping on Bailey's brain demanding to be let out.

Caffeine and chocolate are permanent fixtures in Bailey's office and are never far from hand at any given time. Removing either of those necessities from Bailey's presence can result in what is known as A Very, Very Scary Bailey and is not advised under any circumstances.

Bailey Bradford loves to hear from readers. You can find contact information, website details and an author profile page at https://www.pride-publishing.com/

PRIDE

PUBLISHING